Plumbing the depths of a mystery . . .

The bucket stuck and I put my head back under the sink to see what the problem was, shining the light on the exposed pipe ends.

Something bright caught my eye. Given the condition of those pipes, there shouldn't be anything bright under that sink.

Dirty, yes. Rusty, yes. Smelly, definitely.

But not bright and shiny.

I poked one gloved finger into the pipe, but the thick leather didn't fit in the tight opening. I pulled the glove off, reached for the pipe, then reconsidered.

I had no idea what I was reaching for.

I grabbed a close-fitting latex glove from my pocket, stretched it over my hand, and reached back under the sink.

It was a lump of metal and stone, large enough to block most of the pipe. It should have been too large to have fallen down the drain, except the drain guard had rusted through, probably years ago.

The piece was lodged crosswise, and I pried it loose w̲ pipe and landed in the bu̲

ve brooch, and one I
th̲r, the retired librarian
w̲a, had worn it every
d̲ woman always wears
h̲ch I remembered, she
n̲ why was the librar-
i̲glop of plumbing goo
i̲

sink
trap

christy evans

BERKLEY PRIME CRIME, NEW YORK

THE BERKLEY PUBLISHING GROUP
Published by the Penguin Group
Penguin Group (USA) Inc.
375 Hudson Street, New York, New York 10014, USA
Penguin Group (Canada), 90 Eglinton Avenue East, Suite 700, Toronto, Ontario M4P 2Y3, Canada
(a division of Pearson Penguin Canada Inc.)
Penguin Books Ltd., 80 Strand, London WC2R 0RL, England
Penguin Group Ireland, 25 St. Stephen's Green, Dublin 2, Ireland (a division of Penguin Books Ltd.)
Penguin Group (Australia), 250 Camberwell Road, Camberwell, Victoria 3124, Australia
(a division of Pearson Australia Group Pty. Ltd.)
Penguin Books India Pvt. Ltd., 11 Community Centre, Panchsheel Park, New Delhi—110 017, India
Penguin Group (NZ), 67 Apollo Drive, Rosedale, North Shore 0632, New Zealand
(a division of Pearson New Zealand Ltd.)
Penguin Books (South Africa) (Pty.) Ltd., 24 Sturdee Avenue, Rosebank, Johannesburg 2196,
South Africa

Penguin Books Ltd., Registered Offices: 80 Strand, London WC2R 0RL, England

SINK TRAP

A Berkley Prime Crime Book / published by arrangement with Tekno Books

PRINTING HISTORY
Berkley Prime Crime mass-market edition / October 2009

Copyright © 2009 by Penguin Group (USA), Inc.
Cover illustration by Brandon Dorman.
Cover design by Rita Frangie.
Interior text design by Laura K. Corless.

ISBN: 978-0-425-23079-4

BERKLEY® PRIME CRIME
Berkley Prime Crime Books are published by The Berkley Publishing Group,
a division of Penguin Group (USA) Inc.,
375 Hudson Street, New York, New York 10014.
BERKLEY® PRIME CRIME and the PRIME CRIME logo are trademarks of Penguin Group (USA) Inc.

PRINTED IN THE UNITED STATES OF AMERICA

10 9 8 7 6 5 4 3 2 1

acknowledgments

As always, I owe a great deal to my circle of friends, who have provided invaluable help and support.

To Colleen Kuehne, Georgie's first fan, and my first reader. Your enthusiasm, sharp wit—and even sharper pencil—are much appreciated. Thanks for all your help!

To my fantastic OWN buddies, and Kris and Dean, mentors and friends. And to Kip, who makes the good times possible for all of us.

To Ximena Cearley, for a glimpse at the real world of plumbers' apprentices.

To my editors, Denise and Michelle, massive thanks for the chance to write Georgie's story. Your guidance and enthusiasm were invaluable.

And as always, to Steve—best friend, husband, and playmate. It's good to have someone to laugh with.

1

♦

a dirty business

Always keep a Tyvek jumpsuit and a dust mask on hand. Both can be purchased at most hardware and home supply stores. You'll be glad to have them when you have to crawl underneath the house, or through the attic. When dirt and worse are flying everywhere, it's handy to have a tough outer layer to repel it.

—A Plumber's Tip from Georgiana Neverall

chapter 1

"Georgiana? Georgiana Neverall, is that you under there?"

My mother, Sandra Neverall, the doyenne of Whitlock Estates Realty and one of the more demanding customers of Hickey & Hickey Plumbing, stood in the doorway. Her stylish stiletto heels, the only part of her visible from my position under the utility sink, looked impossibly out of place on the dirty concrete of the warehouse floor.

My mother could turn a simple hello into a referendum on my entire life. "Yes, Mother. Who else would it be but your only daughter?"

I regretted it the instant the words left my mouth. She knew how to push my buttons, and I knew she knew, but it didn't stop me from rising to her bait.

"We-l-l-l-l . . ." She dragged the word out, and I could picture her arching one perfectly penciled eyebrow. "I'm really not sure. *My* daughter spent a fortune on a degree from Cal Tech. I'd hardly expect to find her in ragged coveralls under the utility sink of a filthy warehouse, now would I?"

I bit back the impulse to answer in kind. We'd read that script too many times already. I'd recently discovered I *liked* wearing coveralls and crawling under sinks, and she thought I should wear aprons and serve meatloaf to an adoring husband. Or at least make some use of that pricy college degree.

"And yet, you have." I abandoned the stubborn pipe joint and wiggled out from under the sink, standing up to face my mother, work boots to stilettos. "So, what was so important that you dragged yourself all the way out here to find me?"

She widened her eyes in an attempt at innocence. She held the expression for a few seconds, but then realized I wasn't buying her act and gave it up.

I love my mother, and I truly believe she loves me. But that didn't mean we dropped in on each other, or palled around together.

Or understood each other.

To tell the truth, I was surprised she even knew where to find me.

"I went by that charity house first. I assumed you were there." She refused to call the project by its proper name, Portland Homes for Help.

"I finished there before I came to work." For a moment I remembered the rich odor of fresh-cut pine and the scent of new carpet. The house was nearly done, smelling like hope and the promise of help for one deserving family.

"It's *charity*, Georgiana," she said, as though reading my thoughts. She says that's a mom talent that never goes away. She'd been really good at it when I was a teenager, but you'd think it would lose its potency when I passed thirty.

Apparently not.

But it explained how she found me. The Homes for Help crew ratted me out.

I nodded, bit my tongue, and waited for her to go on.

"I'm on my way out to the Clackamas Commons Development," she finally continued. "Gregory and I." She always referred to her boss as Gregory, not Mr. Whitlock, and I wondered for a moment about the apparent level of familiarity before I focused back on her words. "—so we're going to take over sales for all three hundred units."

"Great, Mom. Really. If anyone can sell those places, it's you. I can picture the commissions stacking up." I grinned at her, to let her know I really was pleased. "But you didn't need to come all the way out here to tell me that. You could have called."

"It was on my way," she lied, waving a freshly manicured hand in dismissal.

Plum Crazy. The color registered without thought. I hadn't had a manicure in over two years—not since I left the high-wire act of corporate competition—but it used to be my favorite color. And it described perfectly the way my mother made me feel.

I turned away and crouched back under the edge of the sink. "That's great news, Mom. Thanks for telling me. But I need to get back to this job."

I really didn't expect it to work, and it didn't. But it did make her get to the point. Finally.

Her tone became all-business, as though someone had thrown a switch. I found her ability to change so abruptly a tad creepy. Then again, it was a useful talent.

"I just talked to Barry," she said.

So she'd come to see my boss, Barry the Plumber, not me. "He promised me the two of you would get this inspection done by tomorrow." She glanced around the warehouse, her nose wrinkled in distaste. "And he said he'd start on the house as soon as you finish here."

She paused and I hoped we were finished, but she had one more zinger before she left. "I asked for you on this one, Georgiana, because I know you need the work. I just hope you don't waste too much time on that *charity* house when you have a *paying* job waiting."

She walked away, her heels clicking loudly in the empty space, and I wiggled back under the sink. Charity, I reflected, was not one of Sandra Neverall's strong suits.

Be fair, I reminded myself, as I went back to work on the corroded pipes. Charity was what forced her to go to work after my dad died. The beloved Dr. Neverall of Pine Ridge, Oregon, had treated his patients for free, and left his widow with a stack of unpaid bills and a load of resentment.

I promised myself I'd cut her some slack.

Or at least I'd try.

The inspection of the vacant Tepper warehouse hadn't gone well. The last tenant, a construction company, hadn't treated the place well, and so far we'd discovered one restroom with some serious leaks, and a stopped-up utility sink.

Fortunately for me, clogged pipes are easier to diagnose than leaks, so Barry took the bathroom and I got the sink.

But on this job, nothing turned out to be simple. I'd struggled with a plumber's snake for twenty minutes before I gave up, grabbed my tools, and crawled under the sink where my mother had found me.

Plumbers, in my limited experience, spent an inordinate amount of time under sinks. Or under houses. I'd take the sink any day.

From my cramped quarters back under the sink, I heard familiar footsteps echo through the empty warehouse. Over my shoulder I saw the worn steel-toe boots of my boss, Barry Hickey.

Lately, I identified everyone by their shoes.

"Hand me that work light, would you, Bear? I can hardly see what I'm doing under here." The nickname fit his stocky frame and brown hair, though I didn't use it often. It seemed a little too familiar.

But sometimes Barry felt more like the older brother I never had than my boss. And it didn't hurt our budding friendship that I made the office computers do tricks he didn't think possible.

Barry thrust the small round light under the counter, into my outstretched palm. "Getting late," he said. "I'm done with that bathroom for now. We could knock off for the night, come back in the morning when you can see what you're doing."

I wiggled farther under the sink and grabbed the wrench handle with my leather-gloved hands. I tightened the jaws around the connecting ring of the drain pipe, digging into seventy years' accumulation of unidentifiable corrosion.

"I can see," I protested. "Besides, another five minutes, I swear, and I'll be done under here." I grunted as I pushed against the wrench, my reward a scant inch of movement. "And we can't come back tomorrow," I continued as I braced myself for another push. "We have to do the walk-through on the Tepper house."

The two properties were both owned by Martha Tepper, a retired librarian who'd left town a couple weeks back. I'd heard she was tired of Oregon winters and wanted someplace with sunshine.

I thought she went to Arizona, though I wasn't sure. I hadn't seen much of her since I left for college, but I remembered her from summer vacations when I camped out in the mystery section of the library.

Now my mother and Gregory were working with Rick and Rachel Gladstone, Martha's attorneys, on a deal for both properties.

"You promised Sandra it'd be done, and she wants to get back to the Gladstones before the end of the week."

The wrench moved again. The pipes in the warehouse were old, but I had the right tools and a whole lot of stubborn.

"Sandra?" A disapproving tone crept into my boss's voice. "Georgiana, she's your mother."

It bugged Barry when I called my mom by her first name, but it was one way I kept my personal and professional lives separate. And as long as Hickey & Hickey worked for Whitlock Estates Realty, I needed that separation.

I'd already messed that up once today, talking to Sandra herself. I wasn't going to do it again.

"She is. When I'm at her house for Sunday dinner or we're visiting her sister in Sweet Home. Not when she's paying for a job, Barry. Then she's Sandra. Or would you rather I called her Mrs. Neverall?"

Barry's feet moved away, out of my line of sight. He paced across the dirty concrete floor of the warehouse.

Barry wasn't good at waiting.

I herked on the wrench one more time and the connector ring broke loose. A couple good turns and I was able to put the wrench down and turn the coupling by hand.

The stubborn joint came free, releasing the end of the outlet pipe. A gush of stagnant water ran into the waiting plastic bucket. Judging by the stench, that water had been sitting in the pipe for a long time.

I dropped the rusty coupling in the bucket and wormed my way back out from under the sink.

"You know, Barry, you didn't put 'contortionist' on the job description." I reached back in for the work light and played the illumination over the end of the pipe to be sure the flow of stinky water stopped before I moved the bucket.

· Barry chuckled. "You're the girl who wanted to be a plumber," he said.

"Woman, Barry. Woman. Your daughter is a girl. Maybe. But I am not a 'girl.' Haven't been for years." I reached under the sink to retrieve the bucket.

"Megan's twelve. Of course she's a girl."

I glanced up, smiling and shaking my head. "Not so much anymore, Barry. She might tolerate you calling her that right now, but not for much longer."

Through the high windows of the warehouse, the sky was nearly dark. I let go of the bucket and pulled back the cuff of my leather glove to glance at the scratched plastic bezel of my dime-store watch. I had learned the hard way never to wear a good watch when messing with pipes.

Nearly seven. I was late for dinner with Wade Montgomery.

I bit back a curse. Barry tolerated a lot from me, but one of his rules was no cursing in front of customers, which had morphed into no cursing on the job. Never mind that there wasn't anyone in the building but the two of us, or that he was probably the only construction-trade guy in the country who didn't swear a blue streak. It was still a rule.

The bucket stuck and I put my head back under the sink to see what the problem was, shining the light on the exposed pipe ends.

Something bright caught my eye. Given the condition of those pipes, there shouldn't be anything bright under that sink.

Dirty, yes. Rusty, yes. Smelly, definitely.

But not bright and shiny.

I poked one gloved finger into the pipe, but the thick leather didn't fit in the tight opening. I pulled the glove off, reached for the pipe, then reconsidered.

I had no idea what I was reaching for.

I grabbed a close-fitting latex glove from my pocket, stretched it over my hand, and reached back under the sink.

It was a lump of metal and stone, large enough to block most of the pipe. It should have been too large to have fallen down the drain, except the drain guard had rusted through, probably years ago.

The piece was lodged crosswise, and I pried it loose with my finger. It popped out of the pipe and landed in the bucket with a plop.

Curious, I fished it out.

It was a brooch. A very distinctive brooch, and one I thought I recognized. Martha Tepper, the retired librarian who was supposed to be in Arizona, had worn it every day, the same way a happily married woman always wears her wedding band. If it was the brooch I remembered, she never went anywhere without it. So why was the librarian's favorite accessory sitting in a glop of plumbing goo in my hand?

After being lodged in the drain pipe of an empty warehouse in Pine Ridge, Oregon?

And what was I going to do about it?

chapter 2

I stared down at the bucket of stagnant, smelly water. There might be a clue as to how the brooch got in the pipe in all that waste, and I didn't relish the thought of sticking my hands in there.

But I wasn't comfortable with not checking it out, either.

As I stood there, torn between curiosity and disgust, Barry headed back in my direction, his toolbox bumping against his leg with each step. He was probably late for dinner, too, I realized, with a flash of guilt.

"Will Paula wait dinner for you?" I asked, dragging the bucket toward the door.

With no reliable plumbing, we were better off emptying it outside. But maybe I shouldn't dump it at all. Maybe I should take a closer look at what was in that drain along with the brooch.

"Already called her." He grinned. "She fed the kids, but she said she'd wait for me."

He reached the door a couple steps ahead of me, and held it while I went through. The gesture was typical

Barry. Hauling the heavy, stinky bucket was part of my job, but holding the door was the kind of small courtesy that was his nature.

The brooch was still in my pocket when Barry locked the door and headed for his pickup. I hesitated, the bucket hanging heavily from my hand. What if what I'd just discovered was important? What if there was something else important in there, and I just threw it away?

"Hold up a sec," I called after him. "Got something I want you to look at."

He came back to where I stood under the faint glow from a battered light fixture on the outside of the building.

I took the brooch out of my pocket and held it out to him. "Found this in the pipe. Do you recognize it?"

He shook his head, but his forehead wrinkled as though he wasn't sure. "Looks kinda familiar, but I can't say from where."

"I think it was Miss Tepper's."

Barry shook his head. "Maybe, but you couldn't prove it by me." He thought for a moment. "Paula might know."

Barry's wife, Paula Ciccone, had taken over as librarian when Miss Tepper retired. The two women were friends, and if anyone would know about Miss Tepper, it was Paula.

"Don't you think it's strange, though, finding it in the pipes like that?" I asked. "I mean, I never saw her without it. She wore it every day."

Barry shrugged. "People lose stuff down drains all the time, Georgie. Think about how many calls we've had where we found jewelry in the plumbing."

He had a point. Just that week we'd fished a Tiffany wedding ring out of a kitchen trap and a ruby belly-button ring from a shower drain. But I figured this brooch was special, the kind of thing that would have Miss Tepper on the phone to a plumber to retrieve it the very day it was lost.

"Barry, this isn't the kind of thing you leave sitting on the sink, or wear in the shower. She wore this on her jacket every day."

"And she probably came in here for a final inspection before she left." He shook his head. "She owned the building, after all. That pin is old. It probably broke or unpinned itself and fell off, and she didn't even notice."

"I don't know . . ."

"I'm sure she's missed it by now, and doesn't know where she lost it. Think how happy she'll be to get it back." He grinned at me. "You'll be her hero."

It was my turn to shrug. "If you think so," I said slowly.

Barry laughed. "Now you're sounding like Paula, and I get enough of that at home! Always has to be a dramatic story with her."

"Okay." I would have raised a hand in surrender, but I had a toolbox in one, and the bucket in the other. "You're probably right. I bet she'll be glad to see it again."

I dumped the bucket, Barry stowed his tools, and we made a last sweep through the job site. Another one of Barry's rules: Leave the job site as clean, or cleaner, than you found it.

"I'll take this pin over and show it to Paula tomorrow," I said. "Maybe she'll have Miss Tepper's new address."

"Why not bring it over now? Join us for dinner."

It was my turn to shake my head. "Got a date. Besides, Paula just might want to see her husband alone." I shoved the brooch in my pocket. "Rain check? Later this week?"

Barry nodded. He stepped up into his big Dodge Ram with the dual rear wheels. "Sure. I'll check with you tomorrow."

Next to the hulking pickup, my thirty-year-old Beetle looked even tinier than it was. The car had been a high school graduation gift from my dad, who had stored it for me when I moved to San Francisco after college. Now it served as my primary transportation.

I dodged through the late rush hour, my mind still on that brooch. Fortunately, although suburban Portland traffic had grown worse in the last few years, there were still back roads around the gridlock of the east side.

Then again, maybe not.

The traffic gods cursed me, and the single-file line of cars I was driving in slowed to a crawl, then stopped entirely. An endless stream of SUVs and pickups stretched around the next curve and stacked up in my rearview mirror, lights on as far as I could see.

We crept along so slowly the speedometer of the Beetle refused to register. Each time we moved, I hoped it would be a break in the traffic jam, but it wasn't happening.

Wade had promised me dinner in Portland, I was at least twenty minutes from home, and I needed time to shower, do something with my hair, and change. The forty-minutes-in-good-traffic drive back into town meant we were already going to miss our reservation.

I glared at my cheap plastic watch, then shrugged and pulled my cell phone out of my pocket. Might as well get this over with.

Wade answered on the first ring and I wondered if he had been expecting me to call.

Caller ID ratted me out even before he answered the phone, and the wary tone in his voice confirmed my suspicions.

"Georgie?"

Wade had used my high school nickname since I came back to Pine Ridge, a reminder that we had been high school sweethearts. What we were now was anybody's guess. We had started dating again, but the relationship was still in that early, getting-to-know-you-again stage, and neither one of us was sure where we were going.

Or where we wanted to go.

"Yeah, Wade. It's me."

"Where are you? I'm just getting in the car. I should be at your place in five minutes."

Every place in Pine Ridge was five minutes from everywhere else. So far. But the suburban sprawl that was responsible for my current predicament was getting closer.

"That was why I was calling," I said. I swallowed hard

and continued. "I'm stuck in traffic, and it doesn't look like it's going to get better anytime soon."

"You want to meet me somewhere? Or we can take two cars and I'll meet you at Ray's?"

I laughed. "I wish I could. I've been under a sink all day, and I wouldn't even go to Mickey D's without a shower."

Traffic surged ahead and I had an instant of hope, a moment when I thought we could salvage the evening. But we stopped as suddenly as we had started. I'd moved about fifty yards.

So much for that plan.

I stopped laughing, and real regret filled my voice. "Really, Wade. I wish I could. But there's no way. We'll miss our reservation. Can I have a rain check?"

As I waited for his answer, I debated inviting him to my place. But it was too soon, and I wasn't sure what he might think it meant. For that matter, *I* wasn't sure what it meant.

"Wade? Is that okay?"

"Sure, Georgie. No problem." He chuckled, though it sounded a little hollow. "To tell the truth, the City Council meeting ran long this afternoon. I could use the time to catch up on some work."

Wade had been elected to the City Council shortly before I moved back to Pine Ridge, and he took his position seriously. It took up a lot of his time, so much that I suspected his political ambitions were aimed a little higher than Councilman.

Make that a lot higher.

"I really am sorry," I said. After we exchanged good-byes, I hung up and turned my attention back to the traffic.

Forty excruciating minutes later, I pulled the Beetle into my driveway and went inside the house, which suddenly stank like week-old garbage, thanks to my odiferous presence. I desperately needed a shower after working in a filthy warehouse all day.

Daisy and Buddha greeted me at the door, joyfully appreciating my reeking attire. But they had their own emergencies to tend to. They wanted out, and I hurried through the house to open the back door. They dashed for their favorite bushes, relieved to get outside.

I closed the back door while I went to shower. The dogs wouldn't want to come in until they were through smelling every blade of grass. I couldn't leave them outside while I was away—they had performed the Airedale version of "Lonely Boy" a few too many times—but they were fine as long as I was home.

Ten minutes later, I toweled my short hair dry. I'd kept it long and styled when I lived in San Francisco, but since I started working for Barry the Plumber, short hair was a lot more practical. I was liking practical a lot these days.

I'd also given up the expensive highlights and tints, letting my hair revert to its natural dark brown. Someday, I was sure, I would have to start coloring it again, or resign myself to going silver. But that was still several years away.

I hoped. I certainly couldn't judge by my mother. I didn't think she'd seen her natural hair color since I was a little kid.

I'd laid out my black silk trousers and pale gray cashmere sweater before work, with a pair of black flats and sterling silver hoop earrings. Instead, I grabbed jeans and a long-sleeved T-shirt and put the slacks and sweater back in the closet. Maybe another day.

The clothes, and the jewelry, were all that were left from my fast-paced trip through the world of high tech and dot-coms.

Those, and the "toy" I kept in the garage. I bought the candy apple red vintage Corvette when I cashed my first stock options. It was completely impractical for Silicon Valley, but it was proof I'd made it.

Eighteen months later I drove the Corvette back through Portland, loaded with the remains of my Union Square wardrobe, and parked it in the garage of my rented bungalow.

Samurai Security was no longer mine, thanks to the double-dealing of Blake Weston and his partners, and the dot-com crash hadn't helped matters any.

The Jimmy Choos went to a consignment shop, along with the Italian suits and a couple of Fendi handbags.

But I kept the Corvette.

Not that I got to drive it much. It wasn't any better suited to the great North-wet than it was to the hills and congestion of San Francisco. But on the occasional sunny summer afternoon, it was still heaven to drive over the sweeping curves of Mount Hood.

I opened the back door, and Daisy and Buddha bounded through. They knew the drill. It was treat time.

I grabbed a couple green treats and told them to sit. Daisy sprawled on the floor and Buddha squatted, his tail sweeping the floor in anticipation.

Close enough.

I tossed each of them a treat, which disappeared in a microsecond.

Dinner was my next objective. I stared into the refrigerator, looking for inspiration.

My mother would have a fit if she could see this. Even now, with a full-time job, she kept her refrigerator stocked with fresh vegetables, fruit, and carefully arranged plastic containers of casseroles. She planned her meals in advance, and she always knew what she had on hand.

That much organization made me crazy.

My refrigerator, on the other hand, contained a half can of dog food with a scrap of foil on top because I couldn't find the snap-on lid, some leftover chow mein from the weekend, half a six-pack of local microbrew, two cartons of low-fat yogurt, a jar of salsa, and a shaker of parmesan cheese.

It was a bachelor fridge, a bad habit I'd picked up while working eighty- and hundred-hour weeks.

Somewhere there had to be a happy medium, but I hadn't found it yet.

I thought about calling Barry and taking him up on his

offer of dinner, but he'd said Paula was waiting for him, so they would have already eaten. I could wait until tomorrow to talk to Paula. No telling how long that brooch had been lodged down that pipe. It was old news—and it would keep.

The microbrew and parmesan cheese did give me an idea. Garibaldi's had been our favorite hangout when Wade and I dated in high school. I hadn't had their pizza in years, and just the name had me craving tomato sauce and pepperoni.

A quick check of the local phone book assured me they were still in business and still delivered. I grabbed the cordless phone, and had the promise of a large pepperoni with olives and onions in twenty minutes.

I thought again about calling Paula while I waited. I glanced at my watch. 9:05. A bit late—she and Barry weren't night owls like me. They were early morning risers. She'd be busy cleaning up, or halfway to bed at this hour. I curbed my impatience and told myself to wait until tomorrow.

I set out a plate and napkins, and thought about the microbrew in the refrigerator. Daisy and Buddha tried to convince me they needed more treats, but I wasn't falling for their begging. I'd learned not to give in, no matter how cute they looked.

Instead, I grabbed their leashes and called to the dogs. I'd discovered the therapeutic value of dog walking when I lost Samurai Security. I realized I thought better on my feet with a couple of Airedale companions. Besides, it helped keep me slender enough to fit in the handful of size 8s I'd brought back from San Francisco.

I debated calling Sue Gibbons, my best friend in the world. For Sue, it wasn't too late to call. It wouldn't bother Sue if I called at midnight—she was a night owl, too, and would be reading a murder mystery, or watching TV, or both at the same time—but there were standards of decorum in the Neverall household, and calling anyone after 9 p.m. was forbidden except in cases of extreme emergency.

Someday I would defeat my mother's training, but that day wasn't today. I grabbed my keys and phone, and snapped the leads on the dogs' collars.

I was on my way out the door when my cell phone rang. I fished it from the pocket of my Gore-Tex windbreaker and glanced at the caller ID, in case it was my mother.

I fully expected her to call and ask how my date went, though I figured noon tomorrow would be the earliest she'd try that ploy.

She had been trying to fix me up with men she considered appropriate ever since I came back to Pine Ridge. Wade, with his degree from a local university, a seat on the City Council, and political aspirations, was very appropriate, in my mother's opinion.

Instead, as if on cue, I saw Sue's number. Well, the number of Doggy Day Spa, Sue's grooming business. I flipped the phone open, wondering why she was calling from the shop at this hour.

"Why are you still at work?" I asked.

"Why are you answering your phone?" she countered.

"Uh, because it *rang*? You know, the telephone rings, a person answers, the other person talks to them? You've heard of this procedure, right?"

"I expected your voice mail. You always turn the phone off when you're on a date. You said you were going to dinner with Wade tonight."

I squeezed the phone against my shoulder so I could calm the dogs, who were now straining toward the door, anxious for their walk.

"We canceled—"

"Do tell!" Sue interrupted. "I don't need *all* the dirty details, but . . ."

"I got stuck in traffic and we missed our reservation. I came home and ordered a pizza. End of story."

"If you say so," she replied. I could imagine her waving her hand in dismissal. "Any pizza left?"

Talking to Sue was like an amusement park ride. The

conversation dipped and swooped like a roller coaster, all dizzying turns and sudden changes of direction.

"Hasn't been delivered yet. I was taking the guys for a walk before I ate. We have twenty"—I looked at my watch again—"make that eighteen minutes before the delivery guy gets here."

Daisy and Buddha tried to trip me up with the leashes as they dragged me toward the front door.

"Garibaldi's, right? Pepperoni? Olive? Onion?"

"Yeah . . ."

"I'll be there in fifteen minutes. You said pizza, my stomach reminded me I hadn't had dinner. This stuff"— I heard her shuffling papers atop the disaster area she laughingly calls her desk—"will still be here morning."

She didn't wait for my answer. She didn't need to. We'd been best friends for years, and she knew I'd be there. Besides, maybe she could tell me something about the brooch.

Still, the dogs really did need to get out.

I stowed the phone back in my pocket, grabbed the leashes, and hurried out the front door. Sue, despite her fifteen minute promise, would be at least thirty. She always was.

The dogs, on the other hand, were past the point of ready, and well into their version of frenzied.

We all needed that walk.

chapter 3

Sue, in typical Sue fashion, showed up more than half an hour later. The dogs had sniffed their way through the quiet neighborhood, done their doggie duty, and were settled in their beds.

I'd stashed the morning's dishes in the nearly full dishwasher, suppressing an instant of guilt. Sandra Neverall would never allow dishes to sit overnight. But I wasn't Sandra Neverall. I shrugged off my mother's nagging voice in the back of my head and wiped down the kitchen table before setting out the pizza.

I'd unlearned a lot of household guilt working hundred-hour weeks in high tech, and I didn't see any reason to change now.

Daisy and Buddha jumped from their beds and ran to the front door before the bell actually rang. I swear, those two can *smell* a sucker from a mile away.

Sue didn't disappoint them. Before I could tell her I already gave them treats, she tossed each of them a small green chew.

"You spoil them," I said.

"I spoil all the dogs," Sue answered, kicking off her sneakers and settling into a kitchen chair. "It makes my work a lot easier."

She helped herself to a slice.

"So," she mumbled around a mouthful of pizza. "Tell me about your nondate."

"You called me, remember? You go first."

Sue shook her head and swallowed. "I can listen and eat. You talk first." She took another bite, as though that settled the matter. Which it did.

Besides, watching Sue eat was just boring.

"There really isn't anything to tell, like I said before. I got caught in traffic and called him and canceled. I ordered a pizza. End of story."

She raised one eyebrow. Why can everyone but me do that? It isn't fair! "Nothing else?"

"Nothing." I crossed my arms over my chest and waited.

"What is it with you, Neverall? You were warm for his form forever, and now you're standing him up?"

"I didn't stand him up. I worked late, and traffic was horrid. And I had a crush on him for a few months, a long time ago, back in high school."

"Okay, so it's been a little while. So what?" She caught my eye, and I looked away.

"I get it!" she crowed. "Mother approves."

"Hey, Peter Pan, high school was more than a little while ago. Try close to twenty years." I'd argue time with her, but I wasn't going near the mother comment.

"Not even fifteen," she countered. "You'd think someone with a fancy engineering degree would be better at math."

"Don't go there," I answered, laughing. "Do you remember who said marrying an accountant would be a good plan because you wouldn't have to do your own bookkeeping?"

"It *is* a good plan."

"And how many accountants do you know?" I settled in the chair across from her and snagged a piece of pizza. The melted cheese stretched out in long strings, until I finally had to pinch them off. It smelled heavenly.

"Well . . ." Sue hesitated, trying to find an answer, but I had her. The only accountant either of us knew was Wade.

"So stop stalling, and tell me why you called."

Sue grabbed another slice, and sighed with contentment. "Actually, I was going to suggest an early breakfast so I could get the lowdown on the big date. But . . ." She shrugged. "Then you said pizza, my stomach took over, and the next thing I know, I'm sitting here eating." She wiped her mouth with a paper napkin. "Which, by the way, is excellent. My compliments to the chef."

We both knew the best thing I made for dinner was reservations, though takeout was a close second.

"I actually would have taken you up on an early breakfast."

She shrugged. "This is better, Georgie. And you'll have leftovers for morning. Isn't cold pizza the usual breakfast of programmers?"

"I'm not a code monkey. Never was. I was the CEO of a computer security company."

"And now you're a plumber."

"By choice. I *like* what I'm doing." I quickly changed the subject. No one in Pine Ridge knew much about the demise of Samurai Security, and I wanted to keep it that way. I had learned some painful lessons about business and trust, and I wasn't ready to discuss them with anyone yet.

Not even my best friend.

"Besides, I had something I wanted to show you. Wait right here."

I heard the refrigerator open as I headed for the bedroom. My microbrew was safe, though. Sue wouldn't have so much as a sip if she was driving.

She was back at the table with a glass of water when I returned.

I set the brooch next to her glass and waited for her reaction.

chapter 4

"That's just weird. Where did you get it?" She picked up the brooch, turning it over in her hands and examining it.

"Do you recognize it?" I asked.

"Maybe. It looks a lot like the one Miss Tepper wore." She stared at the jewelry for a minute, then put it back on the table.

The delicate cameo was something out of another century, the kind of piece handed down from one generation to the next, and I wondered where it had come from. Intricate silver scrollwork surrounded the onyx base, its dark patina adding another shade to the color palette.

"Couldn't be, though. She never went anywhere without it." She shoved the brooch back toward me.

"You really don't treat him very well, you know." Sue had taken another abrupt conversational turn, and my tired brain struggled to follow.

"Miss Tepper?" I asked, befuddled. Miss Tepper definitely wasn't a "he."

"Wade," she said, as though she had made perfect sense. "I meant Wade. Duh!"

"Last I knew, we were talking about Miss Tepper's brooch."

"Miss Tepper isn't a 'he,' is she? Keep up here, Never-all."

I shook my head. "Too tired. Long day, and another long one tomorrow." I gave her a condensed version of events, including my mother's visit, and ending with the discovery of the brooch. "I'm going to talk to Paula Ciccone tomorrow. I want to make sure this really is Miss Tepper's brooch. Paula would know—I'm just guessing here."

"Me, too," Sue said.

"If it is her brooch, I'll get Miss Tepper's new address so I can send it to her," I said. "I know she's missing it, if this is the piece I remember."

Talking about the brooch had brought back the feeling of impending doom I'd had since I first saw the gleam in the sink pipe. "But I'm starting to think maybe I ought to call the police, too."

Sue shook her head. "And report what? That you fished a piece of jewelry out of a pipe? Why would they care?"

"Well, when you put it that way . . ." I hesitated. "But I tried Miss Tepper's old number while I was waiting for the pizza guy, and it isn't even disconnected. I was hoping to get a forwarding number, and instead I got endless ringing. Don't you think that's kind of strange?"

"The phone—maybe she didn't want to get it cut off until the house was sold. I can see that. She could handle all the utilities at once that way. As for the brooch, things fall in sinks all the time," she answered. "You're a plumber now. You should know that." Typical Sue. Right to the heart of things. "You're always telling me about the strange stuff you fish out of pipes."

Sue was saying exactly the same thing Barry had, and I knew they were probably right. I was overreacting. Some days I made a specialty of it.

It took me another twenty minutes to get Sue out the door. I was exhausted. Besides, she kept coming back to the subject of Wade, and I didn't want to discuss my relationship with Wade, or my mother, with Sue.

She knew me too well.

After she left, I picked up the brooch and dropped it in my jacket pocket, deciding not to think about it anymore. I'd take it over to the library at lunch tomorrow, and let Paula have a look at it. She'd know what to do.

At least that was my plan. Other people had different ideas.

Not that I blame Barry. All he wanted to do was get through the Tepper house, make an estimate of the time it would take to fix it up, and move on.

But I hadn't counted on Sandra, aka Mother, dogging our steps as we made our assessment.

We were in the basement when I heard the ominous tapping of stiletto heels across the kitchen floor overhead.

Sure enough, a minute later the elegant pumps of Sandra Neverall appeared at the top of the stairs. Again with the identifying people by their shoes. And this time I wasn't even under a sink!

"Hello?" she called from the top of the stairs. "Anyone down there?"

"Right here, ma'am," Barry answered. "We're checking out the bathroom drains. But it's kind of a mess down here, so you might want to wait for us. We'll be up in just a minute."

He only exaggerated a little. We were surrounded by stacks of neatly labeled boxes and rows of sealed trunks. A large wardrobe stood at one end of the space, its doors tightly closed, as though to hold off any interested intruders. Discarded furniture was jumbled at the other end, but the pile was confined to a single corner. Even though the basement was well organized, it was tiny. There was barely room for the two of us.

The last thing we needed down here was my mother. Her personality was so intense she could make a ballroom feel small.

We continued our inspection, with Barry scribbling in the pocket-sized spiral notebook he carried.

His entire business seemed to be in that notebook, and heaven help us if he ever misplaced it. I had tried to convince him to use a palmtop and upload everything to the computer. He said he could lose a tiny computer as easily as a notebook, and the notebook only cost seventy-nine cents. I'd tried to explain about Wi-Fi uploads, but his eyes glazed over. Barry was not quite ready for the twenty-first century.

Sandra, on the other hand, was already there. When we got back upstairs, she was standing in the kitchen, one hip canted against the old linoleum-covered countertop. She had a Bluetooth receiver in her ear, a PDA in one hand, and she was furiously thumbing the keys while she talked.

"I'm sending you the notes on Clackamas Commons. Please be sure Gre—Mr. Whitlock gets a copy of them immediately. And tell Gracie I'll need her to start on the agreement for the Tepper properties as soon as I get the figures from the contractors."

She glanced over at Barry. "We will have some preliminary numbers on this place today, won't we?"

Barry nodded, and she went back to giving orders.

I tuned her out. It was a skill I had honed as a teenager, like most of my peers. Over the years, my mother had become very good at giving orders. I, on the other hand, had never been any good at taking them, and had stopped listening. I figured if it was really important, she'd repeat herself.

Which she did. A lot.

I followed Barry down the hall to the single bathroom.

The house was tidy and organized, just as I remembered it. The dining room had a heavy table that easily seated a dozen people, and a tall china hutch crowded with antique serving pieces and the cup-and-saucer collection Miss Tepper had inherited from her mother. There was a single bed in the main bedroom, still covered with an old-fashioned chenille bedspread. The closet door was ajar and the tiny closet was empty. Another wardrobe, similar to the one in the basement, stood open, a single bare wire hanger on the otherwise empty rod.

The other rooms, what I had glimpsed of them, were also full of furniture and knickknacks. I wondered if Miss Tepper planned to come back and pack up her things, or just have them shipped.

Either way, it looked like she really needed to have a big garage sale. It would cost her a fortune to move all this stuff, especially the heavy, old-fashioned furniture. It looked like family stuff, so maybe she'd want to keep it after all, despite the cost of transporting it halfway across the country.

The house, though small and crowded, had been kept up, and we hadn't found nearly as many problems here as we had at the warehouse.

That should please Gregory, which in turn would please Sandra.

I tried not to speculate about the relationship between my mother and her boss, but some things refuse to be ignored, even by my scattered mind. My father had been gone for three years, and I wanted Mom to start dating again. I just wasn't sure I wanted her to date Gregory Whitlock.

It wasn't that there was anything obviously wrong with Gregory. At least nothing that I could put my finger on. He was a little too smooth, a bit too perfect, to be believed. I'd had my fill of smooth men, and I'd learned not to trust them with my heart or my business.

I suspected my mother was trusting Gregory Whitlock with both.

"Georgiana?" My mother's voice echoed down the hallway of the empty house. She peered through the door.

I was lifting the lid off the toilet tank, while Barry made notes on the condition of the fixture. It was functional, but an older, high-flow model. Once it was removed to retile the floor, the local building ordinance said it couldn't be reinstalled.

I lowered the slab of porcelain back into position. It thunked loudly into place, despite my efforts to lower it gently. Someday, I swore, I would learn how to do that without making a sound.

"Yes?" I avoided calling her "Mother," since we were on the job. Instead, I didn't call her anything. At least that wouldn't bother Barry.

"Are we still on for Tuesday night?"

I glanced at her in confusion. "Tuesday?"

"Yes, Georgiana. Tuesday. Dinner with me and Gregory? You do remember we talked about this, don't you?"

I shook my head. "Tuesday's class night. I'm sure I told you that."

Barry motioned for me to turn on the water in the bathtub, then flushed the toilet while the water was running. The tub stream slowed to a trickle, and he scribbled in his notebook.

"Are you sure you can't make it?" Sandra Neverall was not a woman to take no for an answer. But this time she would have to.

I turned off the pale brown dribble in the tub, and looked up at her. "No way I can miss my class. We'll have to make it another night."

"Monday, then." The note of triumph in her voice told me she knew exactly which nights I had class, and had maneuvered me into her schedule. I had to admire her negotiating skill.

"Monday," I conceded. "Just so I don't miss my class."

"I really don't see why you have to go to some class," she said. "You already have more education than you need."

Barry slid in front of me and stepped into the hall, gently forcing my mother back toward the kitchen. "Now, Mrs. Neverall, you know Georgiana has to log the classroom hours if she wants to get her certificate."

"I know," she said, leading our little parade down the

hall. "Though I really don't understand why she doesn't just settle down and get married." She looked back over her shoulder at Barry. "Would you want your daughter to be a plumber?"

Barry laughed, a hearty rumble from deep in his chest. "I don't think I'm going to have much say. She told me last week that she was going to be a doctor." He chuckled again. "The thought of paying for medical school had me wishing she *did* want to be a plumber."

Sandra muttered something under her breath. I had a good idea what. Money and medicine were a bad conversational combination when it came to her. I needed to change the subject, before she brought up my dad.

The thought crossed my mind, as it often did, that he was a large part of my problem with my mother. His death had left her with massive debts, and I was putting every penny I had into Samurai Security. I hadn't been able to help her when she needed it, and by the time I could, she was established with Whitlock and didn't need me.

I remembered the brooch, in the pocket of my jacket, hanging on a hook by the back door. I decided it was time for a distraction.

"Hold on a second, there's something I want you to look at." I walked back through the kitchen, and fished the brooch out of my pocket.

When I came back, my mother was glaring at the kitchen sink, as though she could heal the worn and pitted surface through sheer force of will. Barry was looking uncomfortable, and my mother's bitterness filled the room like an invisible elephant.

Definitely time for a change of subject.

I held out the brooch to my mother, who hesitated a moment before taking it. She held it at arm's length to look at it, turning it over in her hands. She was at the age where her arms were never quite long enough to focus, but she wouldn't admit it in public. She swore she could see every bit as well as she could when she was a kid. I knew better, though, since I'd seen the reading glasses she'd stashed in several places around her house. She knew what the problem was, but she was prepared to will it out of existence. My mother, the queen of denial.

"This is Martha Tepper's," she said after a moment. "She wore it every day." She looked at me accusingly. "How did you get hold of it?"

I plucked the brooch out of her grasp before she could put it in her purse, which she had been preparing to do.

"Found it in the warehouse."

From behind me I heard footsteps. I turned around to find a couple standing in the doorway. The man was about my height, maybe five-eight, and slight. He wore a cheap suit and brown wingtips, and his sandy hair needed a trim.

The woman would have been a hippie—forty years ago. Gauzy skirt, negative-heel clogs, her dark hair an untamed mane that trailed over her shoulders. I was willing to bet she didn't shave her legs, but the hem of her skirt swept the floor so I couldn't be sure.

"You found something in the warehouse? Give it to me," he demanded.

I held the brooch where he could see it, but I kept a firm grip on it. "And you are?"

"Rick Gladstone. I'm Martha's attorney."

The woman cleared her throat loudly.

"*We're* Martha's attorneys." He gestured to her. "My wife, Rachel."

I nodded at her and turned my attention back to Mr. Gladstone. "This is Miss Tepper's brooch, I believe. I'd like to return it to her." I put a slight emphasis on "her."

Mom's cell phone beeped, pulling her away from the conversation. My relief when she moved into the other room was outweighed by my irritation at Rick Gladstone.

For some reason, his attitude had lit the fuse on my infamous temper. I took a deep breath, trying to focus on the things my sensei had taught me about self-control.

"Do you have an address for her in Arizona?" I asked, a little more politely. "I really would like to return it personally." I smiled, even though I didn't feel like it. "We're old friends."

"And you are?" Rachel mimicked my earlier question.

I was pretty sure it was deliberate, and I added her to my list of irritants.

"This is Georgiana Neverall. She works for me." Barry interrupted our little hissing match. He'd clearly had enough drama for one afternoon and he was also clearly putting himself in charge.

"We found the brooch in the warehouse."

Somehow, the information that it had been in the drain suddenly seemed important, and I wasn't sure I wanted to tell them exactly where we'd found it. I noticed Barry avoided giving any more details, too.

I thought of Miss Tepper, and I could see her in the library, behind the tall counter with its spinning rack of stamps, the brooch on the lapel of her jacket in the winter, or the collar of her shirt in the summer.

There was no reason that brooch should be here.

That woman would have moved heaven and earth to find it if she'd lost it. It was my responsibility to get it back to her.

"Here's my card." Barry handed each of the Gladstones a business card with the office phone number on it. "You can just call the office with Miss Tepper's new address."

"Well," Rachel said slowly, "if you're sure." She glanced at her husband. "I think we have her new number back at the office. We'll get it to you as soon as we can."

Rachel looked over at me, and gave me a little smile. "She probably didn't even realize it was gone."

"Has she asked about it?" I said.

Rachel shook her head. "It's so hard to keep track of everything when there's so much going on, I'm sure she just hasn't missed it. We haven't talked to her for several days, but I'm sure everything's fine."

Rick nodded. "If you'll excuse us, we came out to check a couple things, but we really need to get back to the office."

Rachel made a show of checking her watch, and sucked in a big breath. "I had no idea it was so late."

The two of them hurried out without checking anything, and a moment later I heard a car drive off.

Somehow, I wasn't reassured. They hadn't talked to Martha Tepper in several days. Something could have happened in the meantime, and they wouldn't even know.

There really could be something wrong here.

It was time I started looking into this for real.

2

◆

something smells here

To keep your garbage disposal odor-free, run a citrus rind—orange, lemon, grapefruit—through it about once a week.

—A Plumber's Tip from Georgiana Neverall

chapter 5

"I'll check with Paula at lunchtime," I said, and dropped the brooch into the pocket of my coveralls. "Maybe I can get Miss Tepper's new address from her."

Mom came back in from the dining room, shaking her head. "I don't think anyone has it, except the Gladstones."

The Gladstones were old friends of Miss Tepper's. They were handling all the paperwork on the sale of the properties, and I knew Gregory and my mother had been working closely with them.

Still, I was the one who had found the brooch and rescued it from the pipe. It was my responsibility to return it to its rightful owner.

Mom held out her hand, as though to take the brooch back, but I just shook my head and left the jewelry in my pocket. After a few seconds, she let her hand drop.

She'd learned a few things about me over the years, too.

"You don't think Mr. Whitlock has the address in the real estate records?" I asked.

"I really don't know. I guess he might have it." Her expression brightened, and she gave me a dazzling smile. Whatever she was selling, I decided, I wasn't buying. "Why don't you ask him at dinner on Monday?"

Barry had disappeared. I could hear rustling near the back door, and I realized he was fiddling with the water heater, in what he called a service porch. Coward!

"Georgie?" he called to me. "I need you to give me a hand with this water heater."

I shot a glance at my mother. "I better go. If you want the estimate this afternoon, we need to finish up here."

She started to say something, but her phone rang, and I beat a retreat as she switched to business mode. "Sandra Neverall here. How can I help you?"

Barry was doing just fine with the water heater, and he grinned at me. "You owe me, Neverall," he said softly.

I grinned back. "I'd offer you my firstborn, but you'd have to settle for an Airedale."

He shook his head. "Paula has her heart set on a Jack Russell." He stopped to scribble in his notebook.

"And you said 'never,' as I recall."

"Yeah, but her birthday's coming . . ."

I laughed. For all his bluster, Barry was devoted to Paula, and if she wanted a Jack Russell, she'd get one.

I heard Sandra end her phone call, her voice sharp with annoyance. Her heels tapped across the kitchen floor, and she peered through the door to where Barry and I crouched at the base of the water heater.

"I have to go. Some problem with a contractor at the Commons, and nobody else seems capable of dealing with it.

"Barry, I'll have that report on my desk this afternoon, right?" She made it a question, though we all knew it was a command.

"Right," Barry answered.

She left without a good-bye, dismissing us with a vague wave of her hand. A couple minutes later, we heard the deep-throated rumble of her Escalade pulling out of the drive.

As the sound of her engine faded, my stomach rumbled, and I glanced at my watch. It was nearly one, and breakfast was a distant memory.

Barry caught the gesture, and copied it. He sighed when he saw how late it was. "I think I've got enough to go on," he said. "I need to get back to the office and do the estimate for Whitlock."

"All right if I take lunch?" I asked.

Barry waved. "Go on. I know your guys need to be let out, and you want to swing by and talk to Paula. Just don't mention the Jack Russell."

"And after lunch? I can't work here without a journeyman, and you'll be in the office." Being an apprentice had its drawbacks, and one of them was the need for constant supervision. I chafed under the restriction, but I had to abide by the rules if I ever wanted to earn my certification.

Barry thought for a minute, then flipped a few pages in his notebook. "The McComb job," he said. "Tell Sean he's got an extra pair of hands for the afternoon."

"Will do."

I grabbed my jacket and hurried to the Beetle. Time to get home while my carpet was still pristine. Daisy and Buddha were well trained, but they would need to go out soon. Or else.

I tried to ignore the fact that my Friday afternoon was going to be spent on the McComb job.

Chad and Astrid McComb were prime examples of a uniquely Northwest species, the Microsoft millionaire. They were young, brilliant professionals who had taken a chance on an upstart company when Redmond had been little more than a sleepy bedroom community of Seattle, and their dedication had paid off handsomely.

They had retired in their forties, with enough money to do whatever they wanted.

What Chad and Astrid wanted was a castle. Not just a castle, but one with a moat. Which was where Hickey & Hickey Plumbing came in.

The McCombs bought their acreage well outside the influence of zoning boards and urban growth boundaries, they hired local contractors, and they paid their bills on time and without complaint. As eccentric millionaires went, they were good ones.

Digging a moat, though, was a hard, dirty job. Sean had a fleet of power machinery, but it couldn't do everything. Some of the work had to be done by hand, and that was what I would be doing later today.

Another fact of the apprentice life: If there was ditch digging, or trenching, or pipe hauling to be done, the apprentice—in this case, me—got the job.

My stomach grumbled again, and I pushed the McComb job to the back of my mind. No sense worrying about something I couldn't change. Better to concentrate on something I could.

Less than a half hour later I was back in the car and headed for the library. The dogs had protested, claiming the few minutes I had taken to nuke a couple slices of leftover pizza and wolf them down was an inadequate visit to the backyard, but I had overruled them.

The Pine Ridge Library was a small clapboard building on the corner of the high school campus. The size was deceptive, though. Pine Ridge had joined the regional library association, and had access to all the materials of several larger libraries.

In that, the library was a miniature of Pine Ridge itself. Outside the metropolitan area, small and seemingly insignificant, Pine Ridge still had access to all the amenities of a large city. Within an hour's drive there was an international airport, shopping, movies, several well-respected universities, and live theater.

Not to mention one of the best bookstores in the world.

I hadn't been to Powell's City of Books in several weeks. Time to plan a trip into Portland.

First, though, I wanted to find out about the brooch in my pocket, and Paula Ciccone was the one person I knew I could trust. She was Miss Tepper's closest friend in Pine Ridge, and she would calm the suspicions that cropped up every time I looked at that cameo, and wondered about how it got in that drain pipe.

Just inside the front door, the check-in basket sat on the high wood counter, a few books stacked in the bottom of the basket. The revolving rack of stamps had been replaced by a computer terminal, and Paula was logging the returns into the library system.

She looked up at the sound of the door, a quick glance over the top of her reading glasses. When she saw me, a smile of welcome spread across her round face.

She tapped a couple keys, and put a small pile of books on the return cart. Her glasses slid off her nose, held by a beaded chain against her ample chest, and her eyes twinkled.

"What brings you here in the middle of the day?" she asked, coming around the tall counter and giving me a hug. Paula hugged the way most people shook hands. She said she'd never met anyone who didn't deserve a hug.

I followed her to the table in the back of the building, where a coffeepot and mugs waited for visitors. That hadn't changed, either. I had started drinking coffee when I was in my early teens, sneaking a cup when I didn't think Miss Tepper was looking.

I poured my coffee, and took the brooch out of my pocket. I didn't have a lot of time, and I wanted to get right to the point of my visit.

I set the brooch on the table, and waited for her reaction.

Paula's eyes widened in shock. She reached out to touch it, then drew her hand back, as though she was afraid it would burn her fingers.

"Miss Tepper's brooch! How did you get it?"

Funny how she could ask the exact same question as my mother, and mean something entirely different. Instead of feeling accused, I felt as though Paula was genuinely concerned about where the brooch had been.

I gave her a quick explanation of the previous day's events. Her brow furrowed with worry as I told her about finding the brooch in the sink trap.

I mentioned that I had found it just before Barry headed home for dinner.

She slapped her palm against her forehead, and rolled her eyes. "That's what he was talking about!" She looked embarrassed for a second. "Barry was going on about something when he got home," she explained with a nervous little laugh. "I was trying to get his dinner on the table, and supervise homework at the same time, and I wasn't listening carefully."

She sipped her coffee, and shrugged. "You know how it is. After you're with someone for years, there are times when you kind of tune them out."

I nodded, as though she was actually speaking in English. Which, from my perspective, she was not.

Paula was only a few years older than me, but she had married Barry in her senior year of high school. She had her kids young, and started college when they started school. Megan, her twelve-year-old, was the youngest of three.

Paula and Barry had been married nearly twenty years. My longest relationship had been the four months I dated Wade in high school. Well, unless you counted the months with Blake Weston—which I didn't. That wasn't a relationship; it was just a lie.

Sure, I'd gone to a college with about the best odds in the country, as far as boy-girl ratio went. The math wasn't the problem. The problem was, it was also one of the toughest schools in the country, and most of the dates I had during those four years had been study groups.

Long-term romances and I weren't a good match.

Which was probably why I was taking things with Wade so slow. I didn't know how to have a boyfriend. Well, that and the fact that my mother approved of him.

Paula's expression grew somber once again and she finally picked up the brooch. She handled it gingerly, still acting as though she expected to be burned for touching it.

"You're sure it's hers?" I asked.

"Absolutely." Paula set the cameo back on the table, and slid into a chair. She pushed the jewelry away, as though trying to distance herself from the fears it created, but her concern was obvious in her expression. She looked even more worried than I felt.

She motioned for me to sit down. I glanced at my watch, figured I had a few minutes, and sat across from her.

"How well did you know her?" Paula asked.

"I practically lived in the library in summer." I tried not to sound defensive, but I felt a pinprick of guilt. How well had I known Miss Tepper, really?

"I guess I didn't know much about her personally," I conceded. "Mostly, I knew her from the library, and from the teen reading group she sponsored. I went to a couple group parties at her house when I was in junior high."

Paula sighed. She was a romantic at heart, and she loved to tell stories. I knew she was about to launch into the story of Martha Tepper, and I desperately wanted to hear it.

But Paula's stories couldn't be rushed, and I had to be at the McComb site on time. Sean was going to take enough pleasure out of making my life a living hell with the moat construction. I wouldn't give him the satisfaction of being able to report to Barry that I was late, on top of it.

I winced at Paula, and looked pointedly at the battered plastic watch on my wrist. "I have absolutely got to be on the McComb site in twenty minutes. Even though I would much rather spend the afternoon with you."

It was the truth. Paula was a friend, even if she was my boss's wife. We had different lives, but I valued every smart, interesting woman in Pine Ridge, and Paula was at the very top of that list. And she shared my love of books.

But right this minute, I had to get in the Beetle and drive out to the McComb site, or risk the wrath of Sean.

I dumped the remains of my coffee and rinsed the cup, propping it in the miniature drainer next to the sink.

"Can we get together later, and you can tell me the story then? 'Cause I know there's a story, just from the way you looked at that brooch."

"There sure is," she said. "I know how upset Martha is without it." She held her bottom lip between her teeth for a second, her concern clear on her face. "She likes to keep that brooch with her at all times. I'll call her, let her know we found it."

"Do you have her new number?" I asked. "Or maybe her cell phone number?"

"No, she was a little old-fashioned. All she had was the landline. She'll have a forwarding number on her old line. She's always been organized."

I was practically out the door, but I stopped and looked back at Paula. "I tried her phone here, and it's still working, but there wasn't any answer, or a machine message, or a forwarding number, or anything. It just rang and rang.

"I met her attorneys, the Gladstones, this morning. They said they'd check for a new address." I kept my misgivings about their promise to myself. "You have any other ideas?"

"Absolutely. A librarian can find out anything." Paula had followed me to the front of the library, and stepped back behind her counter. "Let me see what we have for a forwarding address, and I'll make some calls. Somebody in town must have a phone number for her."

I left her rummaging through her files, and gunned the Beetle out of the parking lot, heading for the McComb site. Unfortunately, thirty-year-old Beetles don't gun so much as they meander. Fortunately, the traffic gods were on my side, and I made it to the site with a few minutes to spare.

Not that Sean appreciated my dedication.

chapter 6

By the time Sean finished with me, it was nearing dark.
Again. My arms hurt from hours of shoveling, and my
back ached from hauling and leveling the gravel for the
drainfield. I hadn't been this dirty since I made mud pies
in nursery school.

Sean had been Barry's number two for several years,
and when I signed on, he had made it clear that he didn't
like the idea of women on the job. He relished the opportunity to give me the dirtiest, most backbreaking tasks he
could find.

I was not about to give him any opportunity to find
fault with my performance. I'd already failed once in a
man's world, and I wasn't going to do it again. I worked
harder and longer than any man on the project, and I refused to complain.

But I was very glad it was Friday, and I had the weekend to recover.

I got home just in time to hear the answering machine click off. I had my cell phone with me, but when I

pulled it from my purse, I realized I had let the battery go dead.

There had been a time when I not only kept my phone fully charged every minute of the day, but carried a second, backup phone. As the CEO of a high-tech company, I couldn't afford to be out of touch for more than a few minutes. Now I let my phone run down, and sometimes even forgot to carry it.

I let the dogs out before I checked the machine. They ran into the gloom of the backyard, sniffing and barking, celebrating their freedom.

I knew exactly how they felt.

I punched the message button, and listened as I dragged off my boots and shrugged out of my coveralls. I'd need to clean and oil the boots, but that could wait until tomorrow.

My mother had called, asking what I wanted for my birthday. It was still several months away, but I could picture her with her PDA and Bluetooth phone, setting up her calendar for the rest of the year.

I imagined her tapping in an appointment in October to shop for my gift, after she finished her Christmas shopping, and I shuddered at the image. It was how I used to be.

I dumped the boots and coveralls in the utility room, grabbing a clean towel from the pile of laundry waiting to be folded. I was either going to have to get better at housework or hire someone.

With my bank balance? I started folding clothes while the machine played the next message.

It was my mother, again. Just reminding me that we had a dinner date with Gregory for Monday night, and I was supposed to ask Wade to join us.

There was a message from Sue, wondering if I had learned anything about the brooch, and did I want to bring Daisy and Buddha for a trim tomorrow afternoon, they had looked a little shaggy when she was here last night.

I called the dogs in, and was ready for the shower when I heard Wade's voice. "Hi, Georgie. Sorry last night didn't work out. I'm finishing up here, and have the rest of the evening free. Want to cash in that rain check? I'll bring dinner." There was a pause, like he was waiting for me to pick up, then he said, "Just call me when you get in. We'll figure something out."

I realized I was clutching my bathrobe around me, as though Wade were actually in the room with me.

Loosen up, Neverall!

I promised myself I'd call him back as soon as I was dressed.

The last call was from Paula. "Hi, Georgiana." Her usually cheery voice was at least an octave higher with stress. "I've looked everywhere for an address for Martha Tepper, but the only one I have is the house here, which doesn't help at all. I would have sworn she talked to me about Tucson, but I can't find an address, and I don't have a new phone number, either. I tried the old one, but it just rang and rang, like you said. I called a couple people who should have her address and phone, but nobody does." Her voice rose until she was nearly squeaking. "It's not like her to just leave without checking in with somebody. I mean, she used to send me postcards when she went to weekend conferences. Give me a call as soon as you can, and maybe we can track down her new address. Or something. Please. Thanks! Bye."

The machine clicked off, and I rewound it to listen to Paula's message again. Although she didn't say she was worried, the strain in her voice told me clearly how upset she was. It would be easy to do some in-depth computer searching, but from what I'd seen at the library, Paula wasn't all that computer savvy. That would be the first thing I'd show her.

After a shower and clean clothes, I felt much better. Miss Tepper and her brooch were certainly a mystery— one that was beginning to be a serious worry—but not one I was going to solve on a Friday night.

I called Wade's cell, and cashed my rain check.

"How about pizza from Garibaldi's? I seem to remember it was your favorite." His tone was light, but I got the sense that he was testing both our memories.

"Sorry! I had their pizza last night. I've got leftovers in my fridge. It's still the best," I added hastily.

Wade was quiet for a moment, probably thinking. It wasn't like the town had a lot of options.

"How about Tiny's, then?" he said.

"Sounds fine," I replied. "Are they as good as everybody says?"

"Better. But you've been back long enough to know that, haven't you?"

"Not really." I shrugged, then realized he couldn't see the gesture over the phone, and felt a bit silly. "How about if I meet you there?"

"I'm just leaving the office," he said. "I'll be there in five minutes."

"Okay. See you in five."

Daisy and Buddha gave me their best sad doggy eyes as I headed out the front door. "I'll bring a doggy bag," I said to assuage the guilt they managed to inspire. "Promise."

Tiny's was packed. The only tavern in Pine Ridge, it was the place to go on Friday nights, and tonight was no exception.

Wade snagged us a table, and elbowed his way to the bar.

I looked around Tiny's while I waited. It was a place I always heard about as a kid, the spot where everyone gathered after work and on weekends, but it was strictly for adults. As a child, it had seemed exotic and forbidden, full of mysteries and magical smells, none of which I understood, but all of which I craved.

Now I realized it was just a small-town tavern with battered and mismatched wooden tables and chairs, a dark wood bar, a couple beer taps, and a jukebox in the corner of a postage-stamp-size dance floor. The smells were no longer magical, just fry grease, smoke, and beer, though they still made my mouth water.

As for the mysteries, I suspected they were still there.

"I ordered chicken baskets," Wade said when he returned with a couple schooners of draft, sinking into the wooden chair next to me. "Strips, fries, and the best cole slaw you've ever had."

"Pizza last night, fried chicken tonight." I shook my head. "I'll have to eat salad all weekend to make up for this!"

"Not by what I see," Wade said, giving me a once-over that somehow stopped just short of a leer. "Or what I hear."

"What does that mean, what you hear?"

"My sources tell me you—and I quote—'Worked your ass off out there' today. Though"—he gave me the look again—"from here I would say that anatomical part appears to still be attached."

"Who said that?" Whom had Wade been talking to, and just how had my name come up, anyway?

"Sean. He stopped by on his way home."

"Sean? The foreman? I didn't know you two were friends."

"Acquaintances, more like it." Wade took another swallow of beer. "He had some papers to drop off, and I was leaving a message on your machine when he walked in."

A waitress stopped at our table and deposited plastic baskets of chicken and fries.

"So," I said after she left, "what about Sean?"

"Nothing much. He came in while I was leaving my message. Heard me say 'Georgie,' and asked if I meant Neverall. I told him sure, since there aren't many Georgies around here, and only one who I'd want to have dinner with." He grinned, and touched my hand briefly. "He said he'd be surprised if you weren't too tired to even eat, and that was when he said you'd, well, you know." Apparently, Wade wasn't about to mention my backside a second time. Which was fine with me. "I gotta tell you, Georgie, that's the nicest thing I have heard him say about a woman in probably two years."

"Yeah, nice." My lingering soreness gave my words an edge. "I've noticed he seems to have an issue with women."

"Yeah," Wade said. "Ever since his wife left him, Sean's had a sour outlook on women. I don't see that changing soon, but it sounds like he's easing up a little where you're concerned."

"Well, I can't believe any woman would stay with him." That sounded harsh. "Maybe I'm seeing the effect, not the cause, though. And you think I made an impression?" I thought about it for a second. "Wow."

The chicken had come fresh from the fryer, but by now it had cooled enough for me to chance a bite. The coating crackled when I bit into it, dripping steaming juices onto the paper-lined basket. I grabbed a napkin and wiped my chin.

Wade glanced around. The tavern was crowded, but our table was tucked back in a quiet corner. He spoke quietly. "Pretty much everybody knew there was another woman. This is a small town. The gossip mill was churning full speed."

"What?!" I sputtered. "You expect me to, I don't know, be understanding of his bad attitude because his wife left him, and then you tell me he was cheating? No sympathy here." I leaned forward. "I don't accept excuses for cheating. Remember?"

It was what broke us up in the first place. Not that Wade had cheated, but he'd covered for a buddy who was cheating on Sue. When I found out, I made a grand speech about sisterhood, and how his complicity—yes, I actually used that word—made him just as guilty.

I might have been a teeny bit over the top.

Since I was still a kid, the drama queen genes I got

from my mother hadn't been tamed yet. I lived in hope that I'd do better these days.

Of course, Sue found out anyway, dumped the jerk, and was still Prom Queen. My relationship with Wade never quite recovered.

"How could I forget?" Wade winced. "But it wasn't Sean chasing the other woman. It was Mindy."

"Mindy? Mindy Tabor? He married Mindy Tabor? And she was gay?"

Wade nodded and took a long swallow of beer. "It happens."

"Wow." I sat for a minute, staring into my beer. "Have to admit, that makes Sean's attitude somewhat more understandable."

Wade tilted his head to one side, and studied me. It quickly made me uncomfortable, and I looked away. Finally he spoke again.

"It was tough on him, no question. You remember how much of a small town Pine Ridge is, everybody knows everybody else's business. There wasn't any hiding what happened."

That was life in a small town, all right. It was one of the reasons I had hesitated to come back to Pine Ridge, for fear everyone would know what happened in San Francisco. I tried Portland while I took plumbing classes at the community college, but the chance at on-the-job training in Pine Ridge was too good to pass up.

Now I was sitting in the local tavern, sharing gossip with my former high school sweetheart, and I wondered how much he really knew about me . . .

"I can't believe you didn't know. You were always the one with the news, the 411 on everybody. You and Sue kept me up on everything. And now I'm the one breaking the big scoop." Wade drained his beer and grinned. "Kind of a nice change, actually."

He pointed to my nearly empty schooner. "Another round?"

"Sure." The word was out of my mouth before I thought about it, and Wade headed back to the bar.

I should have said no. I knew it. But I signed on for the second act.

I guess that makes what happened next my fault.

chapter 7

If I had gone home early, we could have avoided the subject of Sandra Neverall, and her "friend" Gregory. But a second beer meant another hour in Tiny's. The Councilman firmly believed in a "one drink, one hour" guideline.

So did I. I was stuck.

And another hour meant conversation that circled closer and closer to topics I didn't want to discuss. As a distraction, I rattled on about the latest Homes for Help project. Wade told me he'd done some of the rough carpentry when they were framing the house.

The shared connection gave me a warm glow. Or maybe that was just the second beer.

At some point, I remembered dinner on Monday with my mother and Gregory, and told Wade. To my surprise, he didn't groan or protest. In fact, he seemed to welcome the invitation.

"You're okay with that?" I asked him. "You don't mind the command performance with my mother and her pal?"

"Oh," he said, with a look that said a lot more. "It's like that, is it?"

"Like what?" I refused to admit I knew what he meant.

"You don't like Gregory, do you?"

"You're answering a question with a question."

"You started it," he said, not backing down. "And I asked you first."

I gave it a moment's thought, then shook my head. "Actually, no. I asked the first question: if you were okay with having dinner with Mother and Gregory."

"Have it your way. Yes, I'm fine with having dinner with them. Gregory was a big supporter of my campaign when I ran for the Council, and we've worked together on a couple of committees. We get along just fine.

"Now, it's your turn to answer my question."

"Which one?" I stalled.

"You don't like Gregory Whitlock, do you?"

I sat back and held myself straight in my chair. "I don't know the man well enough to have an opinion."

"But you clearly do."

"Know him? No, I don't."

"Have an opinion." Wade's voice was exasperated. "You clearly have an opinion of Gregory, and it isn't positive."

"It's not like that. I just don't know anything about him."

"Except that he's dating your mother."

"Is he?" I studied the foam on top of my beer, avoiding Wade's eyes. I knew I would see sympathy, and I didn't need anyone feeling sorry for me.

"You know he is, Georgie." Wade laid his hand over mine on the tabletop, and gave it a squeeze. "I know it's tough. I went through the same thing when my mom started dating, after her divorce. Nobody was good enough."

He cleared his throat, and continued. "Nobody was my dad."

"I know that. I know she's going to start dating. Dad's

been gone three years." I bit my lip, but I couldn't stop the rush of words. "But he's married!"

"Divorced," Wade said. "Now." He shrugged. "He and Tricia only stayed married for tax reasons, and"—he leaned forward, his expression hard—"I can hardly believe I told you that. It's a gross ethical violation."

"I didn't hear a thing," I said hastily. "But he's still her boss."

"*Bzzzzzz!* Wrong again, Georgie. He's not her boss, never was. She's an independent agent in his office. More like her landlord, if anything. Didn't she explain that to you?"

"We don't talk about business."

Wade let go of my hand, sat back, and took a long pull on his beer. He shoved the empty basket that had held his chicken and fries to the edge of the table, and wrinkled his brow.

"Then it isn't just me." He nodded. "That explains a lot." He leaned forward again, and reached for my hand. "You don't talk about business with anyone, do you, Georgie? You don't talk about business, or where you've been, or what you did while you were gone. It's all off limits with you."

"Wade . . ."

He squeezed my hand. "You used to trust me, Georgie."

"I'm not the same girl that left Pine Ridge, Wade."

He laughed. "Thank heavens! She was seventeen, and that kind of dating would purely destroy my political career."

I laughed, too, then grew serious for a moment. I squeezed Wade's hand, and let go, cradling my chin in my hands.

"It's been a long time, Wade. Things change. People change. Trust takes time."

Wade studied me over the rim of his schooner for a long while. I forced myself not to look away. He had to give me time, and if he couldn't . . .

"Okay," he said at last. "But when you're ready to reveal the mystery of the missing years of Georgiana Neverall, just remember I'm waiting for the story."

I nodded. "I'm sure you'll be among the first to know." I reached across the table and shook his hand. Then I raised my glass.

"To mysteries," I said. "May they never be revealed too soon."

Wade grinned, and tapped his glass against mine.

"Which reminds me," I said as I set my beer down. I dug in the pocket of my jacket, hanging on the back of my chair. "Speaking of mysteries, do you recognize this?"

"Miss Tepper's brooch?" he asked. "Where did you get it?"

I repeated my story again, omitting the drain pipe, and adding my visit to Paula.

"You know who the brooch belongs to, and you can send it to her. Mystery solved. But you know Paula." He chuckled. "That story will have as many heartbreaking moments as any romance novel in the library. Paula's a sucker for a tragic love story."

"Maybe so, but don't you think it's strange that her brooch would be here, when she moved to Arizona? And her phone here isn't forwarded, or even disconnected?"

Wade shook his head. "Not really. You said yourself, she's planning to come back. And people lose stuff all the time. Especially when they're moving. You lost stuff when you moved, didn't you?"

I'd lost a lot of stuff when I moved, just not the material things Wade was talking about.

"I suppose. I never did find the dogs' water dishes. Had to buy new ones when we got here."

"That's what I mean. Stuff gets lost. Sometimes it gets found, sometimes it doesn't.

"Nothing strange about it."

I let it drop. Wade was certain there was no mystery, and I was sure he was wrong. Miss Tepper wore that brooch every day. Even when you're moving, you keep track of the things that are important to you.

I thought about the things that had been important to me, the things I had kept close when I moved.

There weren't very many.

But I'd bet that Miss Tepper hadn't lost most of her life in the kind of crucible that had incinerated mine. And I bet her important things would have included that cameo.

I glanced at my watch. The hour had passed.

"I have to go," I said. The reluctance in my voice was real. Whatever my thing was with Wade—if it was a thing—I truly enjoyed his company. Even if he occasionally got a little too close for comfort.

"I have an early class," I continued, reaching back to slip my arms into my jacket.

"I'll walk you out," Wade offered.

I shook my head. "You don't have to. I'll be fine."

I stood up and a huge yawn came out of nowhere, nearly cracking my jaw. "I just need to get home and get some sleep."

Wade looked skeptical.

"It's five minutes, Wade. I'll be fine."

I patted his shoulder and walked away before he could argue. Saying good night in a public place like that avoided a lot of potential awkwardness.

chapter 8

I pulled the Beetle out of Tiny's lot and onto the street. Even on a Friday night, there was no traffic. Behind me, another car pulled out of the lot, too.

The high beams of the other car caught my rearview mirror, and for an instant all I could see was glare. Why didn't that idiot dim his lights?

The truck—I figured it was a truck because the lights were so far off the ground—followed me for several blocks. In a town the size of Pine Ridge, that didn't seem unusual. There weren't that many main streets.

But when I took the turn off the highway, he turned right behind me. The high beams were still blinding me, and he pulled up nearly on my rear bumper.

I slowed down. If this guy was in such a hurry, I'd just let him go around.

But he didn't. He stuck to me, so close his lights actually illuminated the road in front of me.

I wasn't warm—in fact, the Beetle's notoriously poor heater hadn't even taken the chill off the interior—but a drop of sweat ran down the side of my face.

I rounded a curve in the road, sticking close to the fog line in the hope the truck would finally pass.

No such luck.

I was only a few blocks from home. One last sweeping left-hand curve before my turn.

Suddenly the truck behind me roared as the driver down-shifted and hit the accelerator.

The truck pulled within inches of my bumper. I was sure he was going to hit me.

I pulled the wheel to the left, trying to follow the curve of the road. The truck edged its nose around my rear fender and began to overtake me.

Slowly.

He inched forward, his engine loud in my tiny car, but he made no move to change lanes and pass. He just kept creeping closer.

I hit the brakes and pulled the front wheels to the right, crossing the fog line and stopping only inches from the drainage ditch that ran alongside the road.

The truck's speed and momentum carried it around me, and the world was suddenly very dark as the lights passed me. The tiny VW headlamps looked weak and dim by comparison.

The truck sped away, its taillights disappearing around a corner a couple blocks farther on.

The jerk! He'd blinded me, nearly run me off the road, and then he didn't even have the decency to stop to make sure I was okay.

I sat in the car for several minutes, letting my heart slow and my temper cool. I considered calling the police and reporting him, but I hadn't been able to get a license plate, and I couldn't even give them a decent description of the vehicle.

Looking for a big pickup in Pine Ridge was like looking for a Starbucks in San Francisco. There was one on every block.

The adrenaline rush passed and I started to shake. It

was a few minutes more before I was able to once again put the car in gear and drive slowly home.

Saturday morning came, as it always did, far too early. I had to be in class at eight, and the college was halfway back to Portland. Twenty minutes, minimum.

At least the early summer sun was shining, and the traffic was light. Another few weeks, and the tourist flow over Mount Hood to and from the recreation spots in Central Oregon would clog the highways all weekend.

All the way to school I kept checking my rearview mirror, looking for a big pickup truck with blazing headlights and an idiot behind the wheel.

I saw a lot of candidates, though not one of them did anything more stupid than usual. There was always some fool that considered a Beetle an affront to his monster truck and had to pass me.

Maybe I was just overreacting. The guy last night had been a jerk, sure. But I was tired, probably driving below the speed limit and not paying a lot of attention.

There were a lot of jerks on the road who couldn't wait an extra minute to get wherever they were going.

I shouldn't get upset over one more.

I breathed deep and remembered the calming techniques from my martial arts classes.

Let it go.

Or as Sue would say, "Build a bridge and get over yourself."

The upside of an early class was having the rest of the weekend free.

As I left the college, I flipped my phone open, and tapped in the number for Doggy Day Spa. Sue answered on the second ring.

"Hi, Sue," I said. "Still got time for Daisy and Buddha this morning?"

There was a snort of laughter on the other end of the line. "Morning?! It's quarter to noon. *Some* people have been up and working for hours!"

"And *some* people have been in class for three-and-a-half hours." I wrestled with the door lock on the Beetle. It needed to be repaired, or more likely replaced, but finding anyone willing to work on a thirty-year-old car was a challenge.

"Oh. Right. Hang on a minute."

The phone thunked onto the counter, and I listened to the faint conversation as Sue finished up with another customer. By the time she came back on the line, I was in the car.

"You have lunch plans?" Sue said when she returned. Another one of those famous conversational left turns.

"With Daisy and Buddha?"

"Hmmm. Can't think of any place that will let them in," she replied, "so no. Just you. Smart aleck," she added with a chuckle. Sue generally took my ribbing about her conversational acrobatics with aplomb.

"First tell me when I can bring the dogs in," I replied.

I started the car, idling in the parking lot while I finished talking. Unlike my mother, I didn't have a Bluetooth headset, and driving a stick shift while juggling a cell phone wasn't my idea of a good time.

"There's an opening in about thirty minutes, or we can have lunch first, and you can bring them in about three. What works for you?"

I looked over at the clutter of empty coffee cups and snack food wrappers on the seat next to me. A fast-food coffee and biscuit didn't constitute a meal.

"Lunch first," I said. "And can you call Paula, see if she wants to join us? She promised me a story."

"About what?"

"Miss Tepper, and the brooch. Now I have to get off the

phone so I can drive. I'll meet you at the shop in twenty minutes, if the traffic gods cooperate."

"I'm willing to trust them. Get yourself back here."

"Right." I hung up and pulled out of the parking lot.

When I pulled up in front of Sue's shop, she was waiting outside. She spotted me, locked the door, and tried to get into the passenger side of the bug.

I quickly grabbed up the debris from the seat and shoved it into a bag, which I then dumped over my shoulder into the back.

"Man, Georgiana, now I believe you're a construction worker. It looks like you're living in this car," Sue said, as she slammed the car door.

"Hello to you, too."

"Take the left," Sue said. "Paula's already there."

"Where?" I asked, pulling across a break in traffic, and heading north.

"Franklin's. You remember where that is?"

"Of course. I haven't been gone that long. In fact, I've been in there a couple times since I came back."

"You said Paula's waiting?"

"Yep. She doesn't have a lot of time, but she said you'd want to hear her story. Next right," she reminded me.

Franklin's parking lot was nearly deserted, and we parked near the door. Paula was waiting in a booth next to the front window of the fifties-style coffee shop, and she waved at us as we climbed out of the car.

I debated for about a nanosecond over the menu. Franklin's made the best club sandwich I had ever eaten, and served it with homemade potato salad. I silently promised myself a long walk with the dogs, and ordered the sandwich.

While we waited for our iced tea, I took the brooch out and set it in the middle of the table, where we all could see it. "Wade says she just misplaced it while she was moving," I said. "I suppose he could be right."

"Yeah, right." Paula snorted in a very unladylike manner. "Wade has—sorry, Georgie—the soul of an accountant. What does he know about lost love and broken hearts?"

"Didn't Georgie break Wade's heart?" Sue asked.

I elbowed her in the ribs, and she turned to me, her eyes wide with fake innocence.

"You did. When you left for Cal Tech, he moped around town for weeks!" She turned to Paula. "Isn't that true?"

Paula held her hands up, palms out, as though shielding herself. "I was kind of busy with babies around then," she protested. "I really don't remember."

Sue glared at her, and Paula stared back, until Sue started laughing. "Well, he did mope. I swear it."

"I don't care," Paula shot back. "Even if Georgie did break his heart, it's obvious he still doesn't get it."

"Uh, guys? I'm sitting right here. Could we stop dredging up ancient history, and get on with the story? I thought you"—I pointed at Paula—"didn't have much time."

"It's not ancient history," Sue argued while raising an eyebrow, "since you were out with him last night."

"I just told you what he said, is all."

"Well"—Paula jumped in before the argument could go any further—"he's wrong. Completely. Because there is no way Martha Tepper would have lost that brooch. She wouldn't have left town until it was found."

"How can you be sure?" I asked.

Our sandwiches arrived, but Paula's remained untouched as she answered my question. "The same way I know I wouldn't leave town without my wedding ring. It was that important to her."

The way she said it, the conviction in her voice, sent a shiver down my back. She didn't believe Martha Tepper just mislaid that brooch; that was for sure. And I found myself agreeing with her.

"But she did leave," Sue said.

"*If* she did," Paula said, stressing the *if*, "it wasn't her idea. Not without that cameo. She wouldn't have gone without it, if she had a choice."

Okay, now she was really creeping me out. Was she saying Miss Tepper was kidnapped or something?

"She's not here," I said. It sounded weak, even to me, but I was trying not to jump to the same conclusions as Paula. Without much success.

"Most people just knew Martha as that funny old library lady," Paula said.

She shot me a look that put me in that category, and I felt my face color. I thought I'd known Miss Tepper, but Paula was right. I only knew the library lady.

"She *was* the library lady," Sue said.

"She was a lot more than that," Paula replied. She stopped to take a bite of food, and I held my breath, waiting for her to go on.

"Martha Tepper was the last of the Tepper family. She inherited all the property her father and grandfather owned, and she was a wealthy woman."

The skepticism must have shown on our faces, because Paula nodded firmly and went on. "She owned a lot of property. She worked at the library because she liked it, not because she needed the money. Fact is, she spent most of her salary buying more books and donating them to the library, though most people don't know that."

"I didn't," Sue said.

I just shook my head, my mouth full of potato salad that I was no longer tasting. I was completely focused on Paula's story.

Paula continued. "Martha grew up comfortable, at a time when Pine Ridge was booming. Her dad always taught her not to be pushy about their wealth, but she had everything she wanted.

"Almost."

She took a long drink of tea, and I felt my stress level rising as I waited for her to continue. "She was dating her older brother's best friend, Nick Jeffries, and they were getting pretty serious. It was the sixties, the war in Vietnam was heating up, and her brother, Randy, got drafted. Nicky got the idea that he needed to take care of Randy for her, so he volunteered, and the two boys shipped out together.

"The night before he left, he told Martha he wanted to get married as soon as he got back, and she agreed. He sent her that brooch from Hawaii, on his way to 'Nam. Said it was a promise of a real engagement ring, just as soon as he had a chance to shop for one."

Paula stopped again, her eyes suspiciously red as she took a bite of sandwich and a long drink of tea. She seemed to swallow a lot harder than necessary, before she spoke again.

"You can guess the rest of the story, can't you?" she asked, her voice husky. "Neither of the boys came back to Pine Ridge. Randy was listed as MIA for a long time, but they finally identified his remains. Nick is buried in a veterans' cemetery in Missouri, next to his dad."

She shook her head. "So you can see why I don't believe she would have left here without that brooch. It meant too much to her."

Paula reached out one finger, and gently traced the filigree edge of the cameo. "She talked about taking a trip, after she retired. She wanted to visit Nick's grave. And she had promised herself a trip to DC, to the Wall. She wanted to look for their names."

We sat in silence for a few minutes. Sue's natural inclination to wisecrack had deserted her, and I had to admit I'd started choking up as I listened to the end of the story.

We sat, glumly eating our sandwiches, for several minutes. Paula's story—as Wade had warned me—was dramatic and tragic; the implications were beyond imagining, yet I found myself going there. It wasn't a nice place to be.

I cleared my throat, and looked at Paula. "You're not saying she was *kidnapped*, are you?"

The idea was ridiculous. No one was ever kidnapped in

Pine Ridge. There was that one time back in high school, when Terry Pierce's mother called the police. But it turned out Terry and her boyfriend had run off to Reno to get married.

"I don't know what I'm saying," Paula answered. Worry creased her forehead, and set her mouth in a tight line. "I just know she wouldn't have left without that brooch."

"Wade could be right, though," I said, though I knew I didn't really believe it. "She left all that stuff in the house, the furniture and things. She must be planning to come back and take care of it before the house is sold."

Paula just shrugged, and glanced at the clock over the lunch counter.

"I have to get back to the library. There's a primary story hour in twenty minutes, and I have to get ready."

I waited until after she left before I asked Sue, "What do you think? Do you believe Miss Tepper would have left on her own?"

Sue gave me a look. "Not a chance."

I felt the same way.

We had to find out what was going on soon for Martha's sake.

And for my peace of mind.

3

◆

finding the core of the problem

Before trying harsh chemicals to unclog a drain, try this. Bail out the clogged fixture. Pour a half cup of baking soda into the drain. Add a couple of cups of vinegar. The reaction between the two should dislodge most clogs. If you use a harsh drain opener and it doesn't work, you're creating a dangerous chemical stew for the plumber you eventually call in. This way's cheaper, environmentally friendly, and won't cause trouble later if you need a plumber.

—A Plumber's Tip from Georgiana Neverall

chapter 9

Sue looked down at her plate, picking at the toasted crusts of her sandwich. "Paula tells a good story," she said slowly, not looking at me. "But I just don't know what we can do about it. The brooch isn't evidence of anything but bad cleaning practices. We can't call in the cops—at worst, you've only found missing property." She shrugged.

"And it does look like she plans to come back," I agreed. "But I know there's something wrong. I just don't know exactly what it is." I laughed nervously, feeling embarrassed. "Wade did try to warn me about Paula's stories. He said she would have some tragic tale, and he was right about that."

By the time we paid for our lunches and left Franklin's, we had talked ourselves out of the funk Paula's story had put us in, though I knew the echoes of it would lurk in the back of my brain.

I made a quick detour by my house to pick up the dogs before returning to Doggy Day Spa for their appointment. While Sue clipped and bathed, I wandered outside.

Sue's shop was on the main street of Pine Ridge. Local businesses lined the street, along with a couple of bank branches and a Radio Shack franchise.

Dee's Lunch, its long counter, red vinyl stools, and stoneware mugs a Pine Ridge institution, occupied a narrow store front a few doors down. Dee had closed at two every day for as long as I could remember, and I spotted her locking her door, as I walked along the sidewalk. I waved, and she waved back, her arm thin as a matchstick.

I crossed the street and followed my nose. The yeasty aroma of fresh-baked bread teased me along, right to the door of Katie's Bakery. I have a weakness for fresh bread, and I emerged a few minutes later with a sourdough baguette and a loaf of whole wheat. It would go stale before I could eat it all, but I couldn't decide which one I wanted, so I bought both.

I walked a couple more blocks, glancing in store windows, taking stock of what had changed and what had stayed the same. I'd been back in Pine Ridge a couple months, but I had holed up in my rented house and concentrated on putting my life back together. I hadn't really explored my old hometown, and it was both strange and familiar at the same time.

I crossed back over, strolling along the sidewalk. The drugstore and the fabric shop were where I remembered them, but there was a vacant store front between them, its window papered over, leaving only a sliver of the room visible.

I stopped and peered into the narrow gap in the paper, looking for a clue to jog my memory about what had been there.

The empty space didn't trigger any memories, but as I stood there, the bread warm under my arm, I did remember something.

Tuesday afternoons, after school. Tuesday was rye day at the bakery, and it had been my responsibility to pick up a loaf after school for my father's ham sandwiches. Dad had loved rye bread, the heavier and darker the better.

I would come out of the bakery, a loosely wrapped loaf under my arm just as the sourdough was now, feeling the warmth of the freshly baked bread and smelling the caraway seeds.

There was always a knot of girls across the street, in front of what was now an empty shop.

Dance students!

This was where the dance studio had been. Ballet, tap, jazz, and modern; lessons every week for the girls whose parents sent them to learn grace and elegance.

My mother offered me lessons but I refused to go, preferring to spend my time in the library, or taking things apart to find out how they worked. But I remembered that group of girls in their tights and topknots, clustered on the sidewalk waiting for their rides, and chattering like a flock of exotic birds.

Even then, standing across the street apart from the chattering dancers, I knew it was hard for my mother to relate to me. My father had understood my need and my ambition. He was the one who encouraged my interest in math, and supported me when I said I wanted to study computer science at one of the best—and most expensive—schools in the country.

But Mom never quite got it.

Now, I looked at that empty space and wondered what had happened to all those other girls. Most, I suspected, had married local boys and still lived near Pine Ridge. They probably dropped in on their mothers, too.

One of the things *I* missed living in Pine Ridge was a dojo.

I hadn't stopped training. I still worked out at home. But it wasn't the same.

The empty dance studio would be ideal. All I had to do was find someone with the money to lease it, the dedication to renovate, and the patience to teach martial arts in a small town.

No problem, right?

Even though I tried to put Monday's dinner out of my mind, eventually it was time to show up at Mother's for my command performance.

I dressed the part, in the silk pants and cashmere sweater I hadn't worn on the canceled dinner date with Wade. As a peace offering to my mother, I put on the string of pearls she'd bought me when I graduated from high school. I would have preferred a boom box for my dorm room, but she insisted that every lady needed a string of pearls.

Mostly, they lay coiled in the bottom of my jewelry box.

Some temptations, though, are too much. Parking the 'Vette in Mother's driveway earned me a disapproving frown, in spite of the pearls. Well, it might have had something to do with the growl of 427 well-tuned cubic inches.

Gregory put on his best host face, making small talk about the car. After a very few minutes, I realized he knew next to nothing about me. Apparently, whatever the relationship between him and my mother—and judging from the way he was playing host, it was more than professional—she hadn't told him much about her only child.

Wade arrived a few minutes later, and by the time dinner was ready, we had played out all the polite conversational bits. We agreed the weather was still cool for this late in the spring, that the local sports teams needed to make some good draft picks, and it was good that the high school was being repainted over the summer break.

I offered to help Mom put the food on the table, leaving Wade and Gregory to their own devices.

Walking into my mom's kitchen, full of the smells of her favorite company dinner, was like a trip back to my childhood. A ham, covered in pineapple rings and studded with whole cloves, rested on the counter. Mom pulled a bubbling casserole of au gratin potatoes from the oven, and I could see a tray of golden biscuits behind it.

"Put the green beans in the serving bowl, please." Mom nodded toward the counter, where a warmed bowl waited.

I did as I was told, as I always had in Mom's kitchen, and carried the bowl to the dining room table. There were hot pads arranged on the table, and I knew where each dish went. I ferried the ham and potatoes in, while Mom put the biscuits in a bread basket.

I was suddenly eight years old again, helping Mom set the dining room table for "grown-up" company, before I got my dinner on a tray table in front of the television.

I liked it when Mom and Dad had grown-up company. To this day, eating on a tray table in front of the TV reminds me of those nights. Minus the home-cooked meal, of course—I never managed to inherit my mother's gifts in the kitchen.

As usual, Mom's food was delicious. The ham was hot and juicy, with a touch of honey and sweet cloves, and the potatoes dripped with her homemade cheese sauce, rich with cream.

For several minutes the room was quiet except for the murmurs of "please" and "thank you" as platters and bowls were passed around and plates filled, followed by the clink of silver against china.

The presence of the china and silver gave me a sense of foreboding. They had always been reserved for special occasions in the past, and I wasn't sure I wanted to know what was special about tonight.

I didn't have to wait long to find out.

As soon as his plate was filled, Gregory excused himself and went to the kitchen. He returned a minute later with a bottle of Oregon pinot noir. He poured glasses for each of us, and cleared his throat.

"Here's to old friends," he said, looking first at Mom and then at Wade, "and to new ones."

He looked at me, and I nodded in what I hoped was a noncommittal way. I didn't want to offend him, but I wasn't going to promise to be his buddy, either. Apparently, this was an important getting-to-know-you event.

"May we all be friends for many years to come." The look he gave Mom this time carried some serious meaning. I didn't have to depend on Wade's assessment of their relationship. By now, it was painfully clear.

Mr. Too-Smooth was sleeping with my mom.

I *so* didn't need to know that!

Look on the bright side, I told myself. Maybe he will keep her distracted, and she won't have so much time to devote to making my life miserable.

Yeah. And maybe she'll fly to the moon. My mother always found time to make my life miserable. It was a talent she had.

I was grateful when Wade asked Gregory about the plans for Clackamas Commons, skillfully directing the conversation away from our personal relationships. My admiration for his political skills went up several points.

"Sandra," Gregory said, "is taking the lead on that project. I think she's going to have a very successful retail outlet on her hands by the end of the summer."

Mom's name sounded strange coming from Gregory. To be fair, it probably would have sounded strange coming from any man I classified as her boyfriend, but it didn't make it any easier.

"She's also working on the Tepper properties." He turned to me. "I understand you and Barry are ready to get moving on the house?"

I hesitated. It wasn't my decision when we started, or what we did. "I really can't speak for Barry," I answered. "He sets the schedule, and makes the work assignments."

I glanced over at Mom. "I know Mom requested me on that job, but I'm just an apprentice, and I can't work without a journeyman on-site. Even if it's a one-man job, I can't work it alone, so we'll just have to see."

"Oh, it's all taken care of, Georgiana." Mom smiled at

me, clearly proud of her skill at getting what she wanted. "I talked to Barry this afternoon, and he assured me we could have two people on the job."

She frowned a little, and took a sip of her wine. "There's quite a punch list for you and we're anxious to move ahead, aren't we, Gregory?" She turned to Gregory for confirmation.

"Sure are," he agreed. "We've already sunk some serious coin into those properties, and the warehouse is going to need a lot more work than the house. If we can flip it quickly, it makes our cash flow a lot more comfortable."

"Do you have title to the properties already?" Wade asked. "I should have gotten some paperwork by now."

"No." Gregory's tone was conciliatory. "Not yet. But the Gladstones are authorizing the work on a contingency. If they can't get us a clear title by the cutoff, they're committed to repay any expenses and to cover any unpaid bills we incur."

"The Gladstones?" I asked. "I thought Miss Tepper still owned the property."

"She does," Mom answered. "But she's out of state, and the Gladstones have her power of attorney. They're acting on her behalf."

"What about all the stuff in her house? Didn't they say they were going to move it out? I can't imagine you guys"—I nodded at Mom and Gregory—"will have an easy time of it, having to work around all the furniture to sell the place."

"They hired a moving crew to come in next week and pack everything," Gregory said. "When Martha gets settled in Arizona, they'll ship it to her."

"Did you see that stuff?" I looked back and forth from my mom to Gregory. "There's a ton of it. She'd be better off having a huge garage sale, and just getting new stuff in Arizona. You'd have to be rich to afford shipping all that a thousand-plus miles." I shrugged. "But I guess she is."

"Where did you hear that?" Wade asked sharply.

"From Paula Ciccone," I said. I wondered why he thought it was any of his business.

"Well, that explains it," my mother chimed in. "By Paula's standards, lots of people are rich. I mean, she married a plumber, for heaven's sake."

"Have you forgotten, Mother, that I'm a plumber?"

"An apprentice, as you keep reminding me. For now," she said, waving a hand in dismissal of my work. "Eventually, you'll settle down and get married."

I rolled my eyes. "Here we go again."

"Really, Georgiana!"

"Yes. Really, Mom. Let's drop the subject, shall we?"

Mom glowered at me, but she didn't push.

"Anyway," I said, "there's a lot of stuff in that house. It just seems foolish to pay to have it all packed and stored, and then pay to have it shipped."

I remembered my move, selling or giving away anything that wouldn't fit in the 'Vette. The exceptions were Daisy and Buddha, who had ridden to Portland via a very expensive truck. I couldn't really afford to ship anything else north.

"You never can tell what people will do with their money," my mother said darkly. "Martha Tepper always impressed me as being, well, frugal. Though I certainly never thought of her as rich."

"She has those properties, Sandra," Gregory said. "And you know how much those are worth."

Wade squirmed uncomfortably in his seat. He fiddled with his napkin and sighed. "Can we please not talk about Martha Tepper's finances?" he asked. "I've been her accountant for the past several years, and this whole conversation is a bit awkward for me. Even if I'm not participating."

"I'm sorry," I said, reaching over to touch his hand. "I just thought it was odd, after I found that brooch, and Paula told me the story about—"

"I warned you about Paula's stories," he said. But at least he was smiling again.

"And you were right. It was a pretty dramatic tale."

"What are you talking about?" Gregory asked. The puzzled look on his face told me Mom hadn't shared my story with him.

By now I was getting tired of telling the story of the brooch. I'd told it too many times, and heard too many people's opinions of what it meant.

I gave him a condensed version of the tale, skipping over where and how I found it. I repeated the bare bones of the story Paula had told Sue and me over lunch, without the more dramatic bits.

To tell the truth, the story still made me choke up a little. I guess maybe I'm as big a sucker for a tragic love story as she is. I didn't want to betray those emotions in front of my current dinner companions.

"I still have the brooch, but I'd sure like to get it back to Miss Tepper. Especially after Paula told me how important it is to her." I turned to Gregory. "Do *you* have a forwarding address for her? The Gladstones haven't called yet, but since you and Mom are working on her property . . ."

Gregory took a bite of ham, shaking his head. When he finished chewing, he looked over at Mom. "Delicious dinner, Sandy."

Sandy!?! No one called my mother Sandy. Mrs. Neverall, or Sandra, or Georgiana's mom. Even my father didn't call her Sandy.

But it didn't faze Mom. She just gave him a goofy smile and said, "Thank you."

Before I could recover from that shock, Gregory turned to me, the corners of his mouth turning down. "Wish I could help you out there, Georgiana." I was silently grateful he hadn't called me by some nickname. "But I don't think I do. I know there's a raft of paperwork in the office, but I think anything for Miss Tepper is all going through the Gladstones' office. I'll double-check it for you, though, if you'd like."

"Thank you." I hesitated, but I couldn't bring myself to

call him by his first name. Not yet. "I would really appreciate that. If I can get an address, I'll see that the brooch gets to her safely."

"As I said, I'll check. If I can't find it, I'll remind Rick Gladstone to get it for you."

I forced myself to smile at him, still reeling slightly from him calling my mom Sandy.

"Thanks."

Mom stood up. "Georgiana, could you help me with the dessert, please?"

"Sure." I stood and gathered up my plate and Wade's, while she picked up hers and Gregory's.

Both men offered to help clear the table, but of course, Mom wouldn't hear of it. This was women's work after all, even if the women in question—namely Mom and I—held full-time jobs along with our other duties.

It took a couple of trips to clear the table, and Mom insisted we put away the leftovers before we served coffee and dessert. "If you put things away immediately," she lectured me, dragging out plastic containers and lids from her neatly arranged cupboard, "you can relax and enjoy the rest of your evening with your company.

"Besides, if you leave a mess in the kitchen, it's all you think about, and it's there, waiting for you, all night."

"Whatever," I muttered.

Though I hated to admit it, she was right. When we returned to the table with pumpkin pie and freshly brewed coffee, it was nice to sit down and relax, knowing there wasn't a kitchen piled high with leftover food and dirty dishes.

Of course, in my house, there wouldn't be a mess, either. I threw the paper plates out as soon as I finished eating, and takeout came with its own containers, ready for the refrigerator.

I thought it best not to explain that to Mom.

For once I was grateful I had to work in the morning. It meant I could make my excuses early and head for the door as soon as I could after we'd finished the pie and coffee. Mom prattled on about how "we must do this again soon" and shoved two containers brimming with leftovers into my hands.

"Now I know you'll have a decent dinner tomorrow night after that class of yours."

I decided she didn't need to know that Tuesday was my regular date with Mayor McCheese, while I drove to the community college. Let her have her illusions.

Wade caught up with me in the driveway, as I was slipping into the driver's seat of the 'Vette.

"I was right, you don't like him."

"He's sleeping with my mother. How am I supposed to feel?"

"He's not a bad guy, Georgie." Wade crouched next to the open door, and reached in, laying his hand over mine where it rested on the steering wheel. "He's just not your dad. It'll take some getting used to, I admit. But give the guy a chance."

"I'll try." I didn't really lie. I just didn't say how hard I would try.

"Trust me on this one, okay, Georgie?" Wade leaned in and kissed my cheek, friendly, nonthreatening. Patient.

"I was right about Paula, wasn't I?"

"Yeah," I said. But he was wrong about the story's impact. "And now I'm really worried."

chapter 10

"I just didn't want to know about any of it," I said to Sue. "If I think too hard about Mom and Gregory, then I start thinking about them having sex, and my brain shuts down."

We were sitting in the back office of Doggy Day Spa, a few days after my dinner with Mom and Gregory. "I mean, who needs to know those things about their parents?"

"Georgie." Sue was using her patient voice. "You know your mother's a grown woman, and she has every right to have a social life. It's been a long time since your dad died."

I felt like I was about nine and just learning about sex for the first time. Sure, you knew the mechanics, and even the whole "when a couple love each other" speech that we all got. But somehow it was *different* when it was *your* parents. And it was *waaaay* different when it was someone new in your parent's life.

"We are talking about sex, not a 'social life.'" I tried not to shudder. "And I would tell you that same exact thing, if it was your mother. But you know you'd feel weird about it, no matter what anyone said."

Sue leaned back in her chair and didn't answer. She knew I was right, and I knew she knew.

"Maybe," she said. "So can you fix this computer thingie or not?"

I scooted my chair in front of her terminal, nudging her aside. The display was frozen, a jumble of number and nonsense character combinations scattered across the screen.

I went to work, pulling out the tricks I'd learned the hard way while running a software security business. There were back doors into almost any system, if you knew where to look. My job, the job of Samurai Security, had been to close those doors, and lock them tight. We'd been good at what we did, until Blake Weston and his cronies took my company away from me.

But I still knew where to look.

It took about twenty minutes for me to find and fix the bug Sue had picked up. At first, Sue watched over my shoulder, although there was little for her to see. Most of what I did appeared on the display as unintelligible machine codes that made sense only to other computer nerds.

Sue was definitely not a computer nerd, and she quickly became bored. She wandered out front. I could hear her arranging shelves, restocking the neat rows of doggie shampoo and flea dip, hanging grooming combs and clippers in their assigned places, and sweeping the already spotless floor. If I hadn't known about the precarious mountain of paper on her desk, and the overflowing file folders in the cabinets, I would have thought she was as meticulous as my mother.

Fortunately for our friendship, I knew better.

Sue came back in to the office as I was finishing up.

"By the way," she said. "I forgot to ask, in all the talk about your mother's love life—"

"Which we will never speak of again," I interrupted her. "Never."

"Okay. Whatever."

I wasn't sure she really meant that, but I let it slide.

"Anyway, in all the talk about that subject we aren't talking about, I forgot to ask if Gregory Whitlock had an address for Miss Tepper."

I tapped a few more keys, restarting Sue's computer. "I don't know if he asked the Gladstones, but he *says* he doesn't," I answered.

"And you don't believe him."

"Did I say that?"

"Your tone certainly did." Sue shoved a chair up next to me and plopped down. "It's working again?" she asked, reaching for the computer keyboard.

For once, I was grateful for Sue's verbal gymnastics. I was trying not to think about Martha Tepper, and what might have happened to her.

"Not so fast." I held on to the keyboard, keeping it out of her grasp. "There are a few things you need to know about this system, if you want to avoid more problems."

I gave her the standard Samurai Security speech, the one I had insisted my techs use with every client. Sue didn't know it, but she was getting a top-notch computer security consultation for free; the benefit of some very expensive lessons I learned in the cutthroat trenches of Silicon Valley.

By the time I was done, her eyes were wide, and her expression was awed. "Holy cow!" she said. "You really know this stuff, don't you?"

"What do you think I did before I came back here?" The words were out of my mouth before I thought about it. I was taking the conversation in a direction I didn't really want to go.

Sue stopped trying to reach for the keyboard and looked hard at me. "I wish I knew, Georgie. I visited you once in San Fran. That was it."

She looked away. Her voice was so soft, I had to lean in to hear her words. "After that, there was always some reason you didn't want anyone to come down. So, I don't really know what you did before you came back to Pine Ridge.

"You're my best friend, Georgiana Neverall. You don't want to talk about it, we don't talk about it. But you're kind of a mystery, y'know?"

"Oh." For a minute, that was all I could say. Sue's choice of words was a little too close to what Wade had said.

"I didn't mean to be a mystery, really. There was business stuff, and I was working about a hundred hours a week. Some days, I had to have a dog walker come because I didn't have time for Daisy and Buddha."

I sighed. "Maybe some night, when we've had a few too many margaritas, I'll tell you the sad, boring tale of my high-tech life." I figured it was a safe promise. Sue wasn't likely to have "a few too many" of anything, and I could always leave out the parts I didn't want to talk about. Which was most of it.

It was my turn to change the subject. "So, how about a deal? You promise not to rat me out on the computer skills, and I'll keep your system running right."

Sue looked greedily at the clear screen. "Deal. As long as you let me trade you grooming for the computer work."

I nodded and we shook hands. It was the cheapest security contract I'd ever taken, but it felt good. I had to admit, I'd actually enjoyed digging into her aging and overloaded system and making it work. Deep down inside, I was still a computer nerd.

"So, to get back to Gregory, and Miss Tepper . . ."

I burst out laughing at Sue's words. I was having trouble with the idea of Gregory and my mother, true. But the image of Mr. Too-Smooth and the retired librarian together was too much for me.

"You know what I mean." Sue tried to keep a straight face, but soon she was snickering, then laughing out loud.

"Seriously," she said, stifling another outburst of giggles. "You don't believe him when he says he doesn't have an address for her?"

I thought about her question for a minute, while I sorted the computer discs that were scattered across her desktop. "Next week, we're getting you a couple flash drives. Then you won't have all of these thrown around."

I slipped the discs into an empty drawer. Apparently, Sue kept everything on top of the desk. It was the one place where I was more organized than she was, an artifact of my years in the high-tech world.

"As for Gregory, I don't know what to think. It just seems strange that he and my mother would be working on this deal with the Tepper properties, and not have any way to get in touch with her. He said he sends everything through the Gladstones, but he did say he'd check in his office. I haven't heard anything from him, though, and I really don't expect to."

I reached in my pocket, where the cameo rested, waiting for its return to its rightful owner. "I'm tired of carrying this thing around. I wish I could just send it *somewhere*."

"Why don't you just put it in that drawer?" Sue pointed at the top drawer of the desk. "There isn't anything in there, and maybe it won't bug you so much if you're not carrying it around."

I put the brooch away there and hoped she was right.

Whitlock Realty was turning up the pressure to finish the Tepper house. Sandra had already called Barry three times on Friday morning before she turned up at the house with Rick and Rachel Gladstone in tow.

I hadn't been impressed when I met the Gladstones the first time so I was relieved when Barry went to greet them, leaving me to work on replacing the valves under the bathroom sink.

The pipes were original to the house, which had to be at least sixty years old, and heavily corroded. At first, we thought we could shave a few bucks off the bill by refurbishing the faucets and installing new gaskets. Gregory Whitlock had made it clear to Barry that he wanted the job done as cheaply as possible.

But cheap and fast are sometimes mutually exclusive, and we had finally decided to replace everything from the wall out. In the end, it was the best, and fastest, choice. Though not the cheapest.

From my usual vantage point, looking at shoes, I watched the procession through the door as they surveyed the house. I could identify Barry's battered work boots and Sandra's stylish—and expensive—stilettos. The brown wingtips were Rick Gladstone's. They were almost a cliché for a small-town lawyer.

That left Rachel's khaki-colored negative-heel clogs. Probably not leather, I decided. Her matchstick skirt swirled around her calves, and from my position I was finally able to confirm what I had suspected since the first time I saw her. Those legs had never seen a razor.

The group came back out of the bedroom and stopped in the hallway near the bathroom door. They were apparently talking about the schedule, and I heard Rick's voice raised in protest.

"I know we said we'd have Martha's things packed up, but we have a couple issues."

"We had no idea you would move this fast. We've hired a crew from the Second Chances shelter," Rachel said. "But the storage unit didn't become available until yesterday." Her voice was flat and nasal, and she sounded whiny. "There was a waiting list, and we had to do some pretty fast talking to get put at the top."

Something in her tone made me think her fast talking probably included the name *Jackson*, or possibly *Grant*. I doubted she would have gone so far as to mention *Franklin*.

Rick cut in, his voice smoother than his wife's. I couldn't see him but I could imagine an ingratiating smile and a confident pose. Under his soft voice, though, I could hear a hint of distress.

"This is a small house, but Martha has a lot of large furniture. And there's the problem of the truck," he added. "Rentals are at a premium right now. I don't know exactly why, but that's what they tell me. The earliest we could get something large enough to haul this furniture is a week from Monday."

Sandra's sharp voice interrupted Rick's explanation. "I really don't care about your problems with storage units and trucks and the like," she snapped. "We've already given you a substantial deposit, and we need to keep the work moving on this place. For us, time is quite literally money, and every day we wait costs us.

"Unless"—her voice rose—"you would like to reimburse us now for the lost time on the project?"

Barry's heavy boots came into the bathroom, and he poked his head under the sink.

"Getting out of the line of fire?" I whispered.

He grinned. "If anybody asks, I was just checking on your progress. But yeah, I figured I didn't need to be part of that discussion."

Barry scooted under the sink, and we worked on the new valves for a few minutes. The discussion continued in the hallway, but neither one of us commented on what was being said. We were just there to do the work, and as long as someone was committed to paying our bill, we didn't have a dog in this fight.

Rick Gladstone's voice had dropped to a silky purr, the words indistinguishable from the next room. Rachel was noticeably quiet, as Rick and Sandra continued their negotiations over moving the furniture.

A few minutes later, Sandra's high heels tapped their way down the hall and into the bathroom. She stood in the doorway, demanding Barry's attention by her presence.

Barry gave me a wink, and stuck his head out from under the sink. "Be right with you, Mrs. Neverall." He turned back to me. "Good work, Georgie. Just finish tightening those connectors, and we'll be ready to turn the water back on and test them in a couple minutes."

I mouthed, "Thank you," grateful for the compliment in front of my mother. Barry was a sweetheart of a boss.

"Now then, what can I do for you?" Barry said. He walked toward the door and I saw Sandra's stilettos move back, making room for him to move into the hallway.

I tuned out their conversation and concentrated on the sink. Barry would fill me in on the arrangements after Sandra and the Gladstones left.

I tried to feel reassured that Miss Tepper's move was going forward. I wanted to take this as a positive sign. So why was my stomach still tying itself in knots?

I waited until I heard cars on the gravel. From my sanctuary it was hard to recognize the purr of Sandra's Escalade, but after several minutes without hearing her voice, I ventured out from my hiding place.

"Barry? You in here?" I called out.

"Down here," he called back. "You ready for me to turn the water back on so we can check those valves?"

I was going to say yes, but suddenly there was a strange woman standing in front of me. All that came out of my mouth was a startled squeak.

"What are you doing in my house?" she demanded.

I sputtered. I'm not proud of it, but this apparition with stringy gray hair, a wrinkled housedress, and dirty feet stuffed into shapeless bathroom slippers completely unnerved me.

She clearly wasn't Martha Tepper, and yet she seemed to think this was her house.

It took a moment for me to recover my voice. The intruder bumbled around the dining room opening and closing drawers, as though searching for something.

"Me?" I finally managed to squeak out. "Who are you? This is Miss Tepper's house, not yours. What are *you* doing here?"

I practically shouted the last few words. My voice had returned, but I was having a little trouble with the volume control. It could have something to do with the adrenaline surging through my body, or my racing heart. Fight or flight had kicked in, and I had obviously chosen fight.

"I know it's Martha's house." Her voice was controlled, unlike mine. "Lived here with her the last six years, didn't I? My home, too, until she got it in her head to run off to some godforsaken desert without so much as a kiss-my-patoot!"

She pushed past me and headed down the hall toward the bedrooms. She passed the bathroom and Miss Tepper's bedroom, and opened the door at the end of the hall, into what I had thought was a guest bedroom.

She rummaged through the drawers and closets as I watched from the doorway, unsure of what to do next.

I could certainly stop her. I was at least thirty years younger, six inches taller, and probably had twenty pounds of muscle on her. Not to mention eight years of martial arts training. I could take one little old lady if I had to, but it didn't seem like a good choice right now.

She didn't seem deranged, exactly. She was muttering to herself as she dug into the bottom of a drawer, pulling out a stack of neatly folded cotton pajamas.

"Throw me out of my own house! Least they could do was let me take my clothes. But oh, no! Miss High-and-Mighty tells me I have to get out right now, can't take anything, 'cause she doesn't know what's mine."

She grabbed a pillow from the bed, stripped the pillowcase off, and began stuffing clothes into the makeshift laundry bag. "Thought I didn't know she left the door open, didn't she? I saw her drive away, in that big car of hers."

I had a sinking feeling that Miss High-and-Mighty was someone I knew well, but I wasn't about to ask.

She whirled around and looked at me, as though she had just remembered I was there. "I'm only taking what's mine," she said. "My clothes, and my books. I'll bring the pillowcase back when I'm through with it. Wouldn't want anyone to think I was taking advantage of dear Martha Tepper."

The venom in her voice when she said Miss Tepper's name made me take a step back. Hurt and anger battled for control of her expression as she turned her back on me and continued her ramshackle packing.

By now I was convinced she was mostly harmless, but I still didn't know who she was or why she thought these things were hers. She was grabbing clothes out of the dresser, and stuffing another pillowcase.

"Georgie?" Barry's voice floated up the stairs. "Are you ready for the water?"

When I didn't answer immediately, I heard his heavy footsteps on the basement stairs. The loose stair three treads from the top creaked as he stepped on it, and I turned around.

Barry shot me a quizzical look. "You didn't answer. What are you doing—" He stopped, his gaze moving past me to the whirling dervish in the guest bedroom.

"Who? What?" He sputtered, too. I was secretly relieved to know I wasn't the only one. But Barry recovered a lot quicker than I had.

"Pardon me, ma'am." Barry's natural courtesy resurfaced as he crossed the room. He walked around the woman until he was facing her, and she looked up at him.

"Can't you see I'm busy?" she snapped.

"I'm sorry to interrupt you," he said. Reaching over, he took the pillowcase out of her hand and set it on the bed. By now, he had her complete attention.

"Why don't you tell me what you're doing, and maybe we can help."

She looked from Barry to the pillowcases on the bed and back again. She reached her hand toward the stuffed pillowcases, and for a moment I thought she was going to grab her bags and make a run for it. I was trying to decide if I would have to block the hallway and trap her, or if I should just let her go.

Slowly, she drew back her trembling hand. She laced her fingers together to control the motion, and looked back at Barry, indecision furrowing her brow.

"I'm getting my clothes." She drew herself up, pulling her shoulders back, as though reclaiming all the remnants of her lost pride. Her voice steadied and grew stronger, and she seemed more in control.

She appeared to come to a decision. Her posture improved, her spine stiffened, and she took on a tone of confidence. There was still anger in her words, but she was calmer. "I'm just getting the things that are mine. Your precious Martha Tepper left me high and dry, and *that woman* refused to let me take anything out of the house."

I winced at her "that woman," knowing she meant my mother.

"This was my home until dear Martha decided to run off," she continued. "These are my things, I need them, and I'm going to take them. I suggest you just stay out of my way, and I'll be done in a few minutes."

Barry glanced over at me and flicked his eyes toward the bathroom. I took the hint and backed away. I stepped into the bathroom with my tools and waited while Barry continued talking to the woman.

"I don't think we've met," he said. "I'm Barry Hickey, Hickey & Hickey Plumbing. We're just doing some work on the house."

"I knew your father," the woman replied. "He was a good man. Honest as the day is long."

There was a pause, and I wondered what was going on. I wanted to peek out and see, but Barry's meaning had been clear: he wanted me out of the way.

"Janis Breckweth," the woman continued. "I've lived here the last six years, taking care of Martha. I was her cook and housekeeper, and I thought I was her friend. Doesn't seem like it now, though."

The control slipped for just a second, and bitterness colored her last sentence.

"I'm only taking what's mine, Mr. Hickey. You have my word of honor. You can escort me to the door, if you wish, to make sure I don't abscond with anything else."

Barry chose to ignore the barb in her tone and kept his voice low and soothing. "I'd be glad to see you to the door, Miss Breckweth. Would you like me to carry one of those?"

A moment later the two of them passed the bathroom doorway, Barry following the stiff back of Janis Breckweth. They each had an overstuffed pillowcase; Ms. Breckweth clutched hers tightly to her chest while Barry carried his at arm's length, as though he was reluctant to touch the contents.

That made me grin. Barry was too much of a gentleman not to offer to help, but he was obviously uncomfortable carrying a stranger's clothes. Especially a woman's.

He returned a minute later, minus the pillowcase.

"Do you really think we should have let her take those things?" I asked. "I mean, how do we really know they're hers?"

Barry shrugged. "Sure didn't look like the kind of stuff Martha Tepper wears. Don't ask me to explain that," he added hastily. "I don't know anything about women's clothing. I just know that those things didn't look like Martha Tepper."

He peered under the sink and tugged at the new valves. "Looks good, Georgie. Let's test these things, shall we?"

"That's it? You're just going back to work?"

Barry pushed himself upright, leaning against the vanity. "Paula said something a while back about Miss Tepper's housekeeper having to move out of her house. She said it wasn't like the Martha she knew to leave this woman homeless and out of a job, but she had to move out of the house when it was put up for sale.

"So, this woman shows up, says she's the housekeeper, and all she wants are some beat-up old clothes? I don't think it's worth worrying about."

Barry might think it was nothing to worry about, but I didn't agree. I was beginning to feel that there was a *lot* to worry about at the Tepper house. And Janis Breckweth was only a small part of it.

I didn't really want to argue with my boss, though. I was still trying to figure out how to tell Barry I thought there was something very wrong here, when he headed for the stairs.

"Let's test those valves, Neverall, and see what kind of a plumber you are."

From the bottom of the stairs, Barry called up to me. "Do you see an adjustable wrench up there? I thought it was down here, but I can't find it."

I checked around the areas Barry had been.

No wrench.

"The housekeeper didn't take it, did she?" I called back down. "I don't see it up here."

Barry laughed. The man knew how to take a joke. "I carried the bags myself, remember? There weren't any wrenches in them."

"Hang on, then. I'll grab you one from my toolbox."

I carried the wrench to the top of the stairs and Barry climbed up to meet me, shaking his head.

"I have no idea where that dang thing is," he said. His brow furrowed in concentration. "I know I had it somewhere, but I can't find it for the life of me."

"Do you think somebody might have taken it?" As far as I was concerned, this was another reason to worry. Too many weird things had happened so far on this job, and missing tools were a bad sign.

"Naw." Barry shook his head. "Just got a lot on my

mind right now. I must have put it somewhere and forgotten about it."

I still thought there was plenty to worry about, but Barry was already heading back down the stairs.

I kept my comments to myself.

chapter 11

"He just let her walk out?" Sue stopped walking and stared at me. "Just like that?"

Daisy strained at her leash, pulling me along. I yanked back, and she slowed. Sue trotted a couple steps to catch up, Buddha at her heel in perfect position. Like his namesake, he was the calm one of the pair.

Daisy had never really got the hang of "heel," or "sit." She especially didn't get "stay." Never name a dog after a flighty fictional heroine. She will live up—or down—to her name, guaranteed.

They were from the same litter, had attended the same obedience classes, and had the same parent, namely me. But Buddha knew all his commands, walked at heel without reminding, and stayed calm, even with strangers.

Daisy had decided the rules were for other, lesser, dogs. She was sometimes snappish with strangers, though she was easily distracted by the offer of her favorite green treats. She was a sweet dog, but discipline wasn't one of her best qualities. In that, I suppose, she reflected her owner.

Sue moved a few steps to the side, so she wasn't blocking the narrow shoulder. My part of town hadn't seen any development yet, and there weren't any sidewalks.

"Sit." Buddha plopped his rear onto the damp grass, and looked expectantly at Sue. She slipped him a small treat, and patted his head. "Good Buddha."

Daisy fretted at the end of her leash, ignoring me. Sue watched, her mouth twisting with suppressed laughter, as I tried all the tricks I knew. Finally, desperate, I reached over and pushed down on Daisy's hindquarters.

I got an Airedale glare, but she finally planted herself next to Buddha. Her body language let me know she was choosing to humor me.

I'd take what I could get.

"Nice dog you got there."

"I let you walk the good one, Gibbons. If you think you can make her behave, we can always trade."

She bounced the handle of the leash in her hand, as though considering my offer, then held it tight. "Don't think so. Buddha and I are a good team, aren't we, big boy?"

At the mention of his name, Buddha's tail swept the tall grass, sending a fine spray of dew into the air. I swear, that dog smiled at Sue.

For someone who loved dogs as much as Sue did, and who spent her entire life caring for other people's dogs, she didn't have any of her own.

I'd asked her about it when I moved back to Pine Ridge, but she just said she was "between dogs" right now. It was a sore subject, and I didn't push. She let me have my off-limits topics, and I returned the favor.

I knew she would tell me eventually—Sue was never any good at keeping her own secrets—and lately I had noticed a couple of copies of *Great Dane World* in the shop. I thought she might be getting close to having another dog of her own.

"So tell me about this housekeeper woman."

Sue's roller-coaster conversation had veered back on

track. "Barry just let her take the stuff she claimed was hers, and walk out with it?"

"Actually, he helped her carry it out."

She leaned forward, her eyes wide. "Are you kidding me? He helped her carry it out? What was he thinking?"

I let out a long sigh. "Sue, you know Barry. He says 'please' and 'thank you' more than any man I know, and I bet Paula hasn't opened her own car door in twenty years. He can't help himself, he really can't. I wish he'd asked a few more questions, but it was his call. He is my boss, after all."

I tugged at Daisy's leash, and she sprang up like a child's jack-in-the-box. She had way too much energy, and I was pretty sure which one of the dogs was responsible for the barking serenades when I left them alone.

"Let's keep walking," I said, taking the lead. "We promised ourselves at least a mile every day, remember? We won't get it standing around here flapping our jaws."

Sue groaned. "Slave driver." She clicked her tongue at Buddha, and he immediately stood up and assumed the perfect "heel" position.

I was tempted to remind Sue of the Dane magazines. If my guess was right, she was going to have some serious walking in her future, and it wouldn't be because of me.

"Traitor," I muttered at Buddha. He behaved fine for me, but I had never been able to get that clicking noise to work, and Sue knew it.

"So what did she take?"

I shrugged. "I didn't see it all. She had a couple of old pillowcases off the bed, and she stuffed them full of clothes. Barry said they were things that 'didn't look like the kind of stuff Martha Tepper wears,' but he couldn't explain what he meant by that. Swore he didn't know anything about women's clothing, and changed the subject.

"He also said Paula told him something about Miss Tepper's housekeeper having to move out because the house was for sale."

We crossed the street, hurrying in the growing dusk.

Walking the dogs after work had a few drawbacks, chief among them being the unlighted streets. It wouldn't be really dark for another hour, but we were still careful.

"The worst part, though, was that she kept talking about 'that woman' who made her move out." My heart raced a little at the memory, and I felt my face redden. I hoped it was dark enough that Sue wouldn't notice.

"Why was that so bad?"

"She said the woman threw her out, and wouldn't even let her take her things. She told me she saw her drive away, and that was when she came in the house, because she knew it was unlocked."

I stopped and fiddled with the leash. It was twisted, though not badly. I was stalling, and I knew it. Worse, Sue knew it and she called me on it.

"And? Get to the point, Neverall!"

"It was my mother." There, I'd said it.

"Your mother? You said she was there, but what did she have to do with any of this?"

"She was 'that woman.' I know she was. She and Gregory had just left, and this Janis person said she saw her leave. It would be just like them to throw her out of her house the minute they signed the deal with the Gladstones. Besides"—the misery I felt when I considered my mother's heartless behavior crept into my voice—"Barry said it wouldn't be like Miss Tepper to leave Janis without a job or a place to live. The Gladstones were supposed to be acting on Miss Tepper's behalf. It had to be Sandra and Gregory."

I sneered the last name, my animosity toward Mr. Too-Smooth Gregory Whitlock growing by an order of magnitude. My mother's attitude regarding charity was lousy, but I blamed Gregory for this one. He had made the deal, and I was sure it was his idea to throw Janis out.

"She sounds really angry, maybe even a little unhinged, from the way you describe her."

We reached my house and crossed the damp lawn to the front door. Daisy strained at the leash as I fished the house key from my pocket.

There was a faint whiff of expensive perfume. I recognized it as Joy, my mother's favorite. That was when I noticed the small, cream-colored envelope stuck in the door.

Sandra had been here.

I sighed with relief, and thanked my lucky stars that Sue and I had taken the long way back. Since I could still smell her perfume, I had probably missed her by only a couple minutes.

I wondered how I had missed seeing the Escalade.

I grabbed the envelope and pushed the door open.

Once inside, the dogs were anxious to get to their water dishes. Sue and I quickly unclipped their leashes and let them go.

They ran into the kitchen. Their trimmed nails made only the tiniest sound against the worn linoleum of the kitchen floor, quickly replaced by the slurping and lapping as they drank greedily from their dishes.

"What's that?" Sue asked, pointing to the envelope in my hand. She took Daisy's leash from me and hung it on the hook behind the front door, along with Buddha's.

"I don't know. Something from my mother, I think." I put the envelope to my nose, and sniffed. "It smells of her perfume. I think all her stationery does."

It was the envelope I had smelled. So maybe I had missed her by more than a few minutes.

Either way, I was relieved. I wasn't quite ready to talk to "that woman" yet.

"You can't read it with your nose, Georgie." Sue rolled her eyes. "Why don't you try, oh, I don't know, *opening* it?"

Sue plopped onto my secondhand sofa. The floral cushions sagged slightly, and she sank back. The sofa was cheap and a bit ugly, like most of my mismatched furniture, but comfortable. It had cost less to buy it at the Salvation Army than it would have to ship the leather sectional I never used from my San Francisco apartment.

The dogs finished their slurping and trotted back into the living room, muzzles damp. Buddha curled into the doggy bed in the corner and Daisy spread out on the braided rug in front of the fireplace.

I didn't often have an actual fire, but Daisy had adopted that as her spot the minute we walked into our new home, and she was eternally optimistic that I might light a fire someday. I wasn't sure how she knew about fireplaces, but she did.

"I'm wait-ting," Sue singsonged.

"It's addressed to me," I replied. "Not you."

"Ah, but a note from your mother. Not a phone call, or an e-mail, or a message on your machine. A real, hand-written note. That's got to be pretty important."

She snickered. "Maybe it's a wedding invitation. Something personal and subdued. Just right for a second marriage."

"We aren't talking about that, remember?" I glared at Sue.

"I'm not talking about her 'love life,' as you so delicately put it. I am talking about Gregory making an honest woman of her." She sighed dramatically. "Imagine how romantic. Lonely widow falls for her rich boss."

I stomped across the room and dropped heavily into the club chair next to the sofa. "There are so many things wrong with that, I don't know where to start.

"First off, my mother isn't a lonely widow. She's got tons of friends, and she's busy all the time. Second, Whitlock might have money, but he doesn't fit my mother's definition of rich. And third, I don't think she needs his money, anyway."

"Aha! But you don't know that, do you? She just might need his money. You don't talk about finances and business with her, do you, any more than you do with me?"

I bit my lip. She was right, I didn't talk to my mother about money anymore. Not since the disastrous time when I had offered, too late, to help her out.

"It's complicated," I muttered.

"I know it is," Sue said, one finger tapping against her closed lips.

"Your mom is a stubborn woman. I know that. She didn't want to admit she needed help when your dad died, and she refused what was offered. I know she told a couple people she wouldn't take 'charity,' no matter how they tried."

That I understood. Mom had barely admitted how deeply in debt she was and I hadn't pried. That first six months, when things were the worst, I was pouring every penny into my business, sleeping in my tiny office to save paying for a San Francisco apartment, and showering at the Y.

Weeks later, my first fat contract in my hand, and a large check in the bank, I called to ask if Mom needed anything. She'd been quick to let me know she was doing 'just fine,' and didn't need anything from me.

Her new job, she said, was going very well, and she could take care of herself. She said she had money of her own, and she didn't need to take charity from her daughter.

As surprising as it was, I found out it was true. Who would have suspected that Sandra Myers Neverall, who only ever wanted to be a wife and mother, would have an incredible talent for business? She seemed to be able to match buyer and property with pinpoint accuracy, and her career had taken off.

No, whatever else there was between them, she didn't need Gregory Whitlock's money.

"Hello? Earth to Georgie? Are you in there?"

I gave myself a little shake, throwing off the memories. How much my life had changed in the last few months!

"So, are you going to open that, or not?" She gestured at the envelope I still held in my hand. "Or do I have to do it for you?"

I pulled the envelope back against my chest. "I'll open it, if it'll get you to stop yelling at me. Okay?"

Sue nodded and sat back, propping her sneakers on the edge of the ancient steamer trunk that served as a coffee table. "So? Open it already!"

Reluctantly, I slid one finger under the flap of the envelope. Inside there was a single sheet of my mother's monogrammed note paper, folded in half.

I pulled the note out of the envelope and scanned the stick-straight lines of my mother's precise handwriting.

At first, I couldn't believe it. Then I laughed out loud.

"What's so funny?" Sue sprang across the table, reaching for the note I held in my hand.

I pulled it away, refusing to let her see the message. "You are not going to believe this!" I choked out, still laughing.

"What?!" Sue tried again to grab the note, but I wouldn't let go.

"All that, that whole conversation." I gasped. "Over this!"

I finally handed over the note, which read:

Gregory and I are headed for Tiny's for a quick bite. Thought you might want to join us, but you weren't home. If you're back before 8, please meet us there.

Love,
Mom

Sue glanced at her watch, and jumped off the sofa. Buddha looked up from his bed, alerted by her sudden motion. "I better run then," she said. "It's already a quarter 'til."

"Why?" I lounged back against the well-worn leather of the chair. It had been my dad's, the one he kept in his den at home. I had talked my mother out of it when I moved to Pine Ridge, and it was my favorite.

"Well, you need to go talk to them, don't you?"

"About what?" My voice was sharp, and I swallowed my temper. I wasn't really mad at Sue, and I shouldn't take it out on her. "I really don't have anything to say to them."

"How about: There's a crazy woman running around Martha Tepper's house, claiming you threw her out and wouldn't give her her clothes? Something like that?"

I shrugged and burrowed deeper in the chair. "I don't think it matters. She seemed pretty harmless."

"You said yourself she was yelling and throwing stuff around. Who knows if she'll come back for more stuff, or what."

"That's their problem. I am not getting into their business, Sue. I think what they did stinks, and I don't want anything to do with it. I'm just there to work on the plumbing, and that's it."

Sue sat back down and we both were quiet for several minutes. Daisy wandered over to me, begging for pets, and I sat there stroking her coat and trying not to think about my mother, and Gregory, and Janis Breckweth, and Martha Tepper.

And how the brooch that rested in Sue's desk drawer at Doggy Day Spa had ended up in the drain of an abandoned warehouse.

chapter 12

Sue cleared her throat a couple times, like she was going to say something, but then she didn't. The third time, though, I couldn't ignore her.

"What?"

"I didn't say anything."

"I know you didn't. But you're *thinking* really loud and I want to know what about."

"It's nothing," she protested. "I just . . ." She shook her head, refusing to look at me. "No."

"Just what?" I stood up and paced along the living room wall, then turned into the kitchen. "You keep sighing and clearing your throat," I called back over my shoulder. "Maybe a beer would help."

"Not for me," she called back. I heard her get up from the sofa and come in the kitchen with me. "But I could use a cup of tea, if you have some."

I dug around in the cupboard and came up with a tiny canister of orange spice tea bags. We heated mugs of water in the microwave and sat facing each other at the tiny kitchen table.

"Now," I said, "tell me what it is that's bugging you."

"Well, it's like this." Sue stirred her tea and took a sip before she looked up at me.

"Georgie, what if Paula is right about Miss Tepper? What if she didn't leave town by her own choice?"

Sue's eyes were bright and her hand shook a little when she picked up her tea. She was upset, unnerved.

"I do have to admit, there are a lot of questions." I took a long sip of tea, grateful for the delay. Finally, I looked back at Sue.

"I remember Miss Tepper, like Paula says, as the library lady. I didn't know much about her personal life, and maybe now I wish I did. But she never left anybody out. Remember sophomore year, when she helped coach the debate team while Mrs. Reynolds was on maternity leave?"

Sue nodded, and I went on. "Every time there was an away meet, if somebody was having money trouble at home, she managed to find a 'sponsor' to help with the cost of the trip. Now I wonder if the sponsor was Martha Tepper, dipping into her own funds. Someone like that wouldn't leave a live-in housekeeper without a job or a home, with no warning. That's completely out of character for her. My mother can call it charity and sneer, but there were a lot of kids that benefited from her help."

"Wasn't Wade on the debate team with you?"

"Yeah, why?" For a second I thought it was another one of Sue's detours, but then I made the connection. "Wait! Yes he was, and he got a lot of sponsorship that year. It was right after his folks split up."

"Right," Sue said. "I think there were some serious money problems when his dad left. His mom wouldn't have been able to afford any extras, I'll bet."

"And Miss Tepper came through for him. I wonder if that's what made him so upset the other night?"

Sue waved a hand in my face. "Upset? Wade was upset about something, and you didn't tell me? Come on, Neverall, I count on you for my vicarious romance here."

"It wasn't like that," I said. I told her about the conversation at my mother's house, how Martha Tepper's finances had come up, and Wade's discomfort with the subject.

"Now I wonder," I said, "if he knew Martha Tepper was his sponsor. That would explain why he got so tense when the subject of her finances came up."

"Or it could be what he said," Sue argued. "The man really does take his work seriously, Georgie. He knows more about the finances of most everyone in town than anyone, except Brian at the bank. And neither one of them is about to give away anything about their customers."

"Whatever." I waved away her comments. "But we know Martha Tepper wasn't stingy. My mother says she thought of her as frugal, and that could be true. She didn't live in luxury. But she was generous when it counted. And I think that would include Janis."

Sue nodded her agreement.

"She was always considerate of people's feelings, too. None of the kids who got sponsors ever felt like they were getting special treatment. I don't know how she managed that," I said, "but she did.

"So she would have been sure to say her good-byes."

"Especially to Paula," Sue added. "She visited the library almost every day after she retired. She'd stop in, have a cup of coffee with Paula, and take a walk down Main Street before she went home.

"You know what we're saying here, don't you, Georgie?"

I bit my lip. I didn't want to say it out loud but knew I had to.

"Yes. I do. We're saying something bad happened to Martha Tepper. We're saying she was kidnapped. Or worse."

4

◦

when in doubt, improvise

If the chain on your toilet flapper breaks, and you can't get to the hardware store for a replacement, use a chain of paper clips as a temporary fix. Adjust the number of clips in the chain to reach the desired length.

—A Plumber's Tip from Georgiana Neverall

chapter 13

"Worse, Georgie. We're saying worse, and you know we are." Sue looked grim, and I was sure I wasn't any better. "The question is," she went on, "who benefits if she never comes back?"

I didn't have to think about it. I knew who stood to gain the most if Martha Tepper never returned to Pine Ridge. "Gregory Whitlock."

"You don't mean that!"

Sue jumped up and came over to the sink, where I'd started washing dishes. She pulled my hands out of the soapy water, and held them in hers. "Just because the guy is sleeping with your mother—"

I yanked my hands away. "Which you promised never to mention again."

"That was before you started accusing him of being some kind of criminal mastermind." She held up her hands, blocking my protest. Drops of soap bubbles dripped from her palms. "I get that you don't like him, and I know you have your reasons. But there's a big jump from not liking to accusing him of a crime."

"I know men like that," I said. My voice shook with suppressed anger. I was dangerously close to subjects I refused to talk about, but I couldn't back down. "They expect everybody to give them whatever they want. If you don't give it to them, they take it anyway. They're ruthless, Sue. They don't care about anyone or anything but themselves.

"And they don't take no for an answer." I swallowed hard, forcing myself to calm down, to bury the anger. "If Gregory Whitlock wanted to develop that property and Martha Tepper said no, he'd find a way to get what he wanted.

"No matter who it hurt."

Sue's eyes narrowed, and she looked me up and down. "Okay, Georgie. Something bad happened to you when you were gone. I know that. You won't talk about it, and I accept that, too. But that doesn't give you the right to jump to conclusions about Gregory Whitlock. It just doesn't."

She took a step toward me, and gathered me into her arms, hugging me hard and patting my back at the same time. "I know you'll tell me someday," she said lightly.

Sue released me and leaned against the counter. She crossed her arms over her chest and stared at the floor. "Actually," she said, "I was thinking of someone else. That housekeeper, Janis. What if she knew Martha Tepper was serious about leaving Pine Ridge? She'd lose her job and her home—which, yes, she did—but if she was going to lose it anyway, she might have been pretty angry about it.

"And she would have had a key, if she lived there."

I rinsed the mugs, and set them on the counter. Sue grabbed a dish towel, and started drying.

"But she said she had waited for someone to leave the door unlocked," I pointed out. "So that would imply that she doesn't have one anymore."

"Right." Sue put the mugs back in the cupboard and reached for the wet spoons. "So maybe she waited until she thought she could get in, and didn't realize that there were still people in the house. Maybe there's something hidden in the house, and she wanted to get rid of it before anyone found it?"

"She seemed harmless," I protested, unwilling to give up my suspicions of Gregory, "and all she took were some old clothes."

"That's all you saw."

"She wasn't there very long . . ."

"So you saw her before she could take anything. Doesn't mean she wasn't going to." She tossed the spoons into the silverware drawer and shoved it closed with her hip. "Admit it, she's a better suspect"—she choked a little on the word, then forged ahead—"than Gregory."

"But she's an old woman!"

"Not that old," Sue said. "And she was desperate. People, even women, will do crazy things when they're desperate, Georgie."

I didn't tell Sue how right she was. I had been willing to do almost anything to save my company and my reputation. Turned out, there were some things I wouldn't do that Blake Weston and his cronies would. Yeah, I knew a little something about desperate people.

"Gregory Whitlock isn't desperate. And desperate people are a lot more dangerous than greedy ones, if you ask me."

I bit my tongue to keep from saying I hadn't asked her. I knew there was some truth to what she said, even though I wanted it to be Gregory. It would get him out of my mother's life once and for all.

And why did I care who was or wasn't in my mother's life? Because I knew, no matter how crazy and annoyed I got at Sandra Neverall, she was still my mother, and I loved her.

"So, say she might be a suspect. Might," I emphasized. "What do we do about it?"

We looked at each other for a moment, then said in unison, "Paula."

She would know about Janis.

When I checked in at the Hickey & Hickey office the next morning, I got an unpleasant surprise. Barry and

Paula were gone for a couple days, a family emergency of some kind.

The work on the Tepper house was temporarily suspended, and I was reassigned to the McComb site with Sean.

I groaned. The thought of more digging and pipe hauling was bad enough. But it also meant we couldn't ask Paula about Janis until she got back.

It also meant the Tepper house would be empty for the next two days. It was an open invitation for someone who wanted to recover evidence hidden in the house.

I checked the job board one more time, lingering over the hastily erased assignments. When Angie, the office girl, turned her back, I snagged a key from the Peg-Board. Hook number 3, the one that corresponded to job number 3, Tepper.

So maybe it wasn't the smartest idea. But Sue and I, and Paula, were the only ones in town who seemed to be bothered by Martha Tepper's disappearance. With Paula gone, it was just Sue and I.

If there was anything in that house, maybe we could find it first, before anybody had a chance to destroy evidence. Well, "evidence" might be overstating the case, but I was starting to believe that there were clues to Martha Tepper's disappearance in her house, and I didn't want them destroyed.

I was due at the McComb site, but I took a quick detour on the way to my car. Doggy Day Spa was only a block away from Hickey & Hickey, and I hurried along the sidewalk.

"Got a minute?" I said to Sue, as I walked in the front door. "I'm on my way to work"—I glanced meaningfully at my battered watch—"but it's important."

Sue motioned me over next to the washing station, where a yellow Labrador turned sad eyes on me. "Her owner won't be back for another few minutes," she said, giving the dog a pat. "He can't stand to watch her get bathed, because he says she looks pathetic."

I had to agree with the missing owner. Labs were really good at the sad puppy eyes, and this one was an expert.

"So, what's so important you'd risk being late to work?"

"Paula's out of town for a couple days," I whispered, then felt foolish. Who was going to overhear me, the dog?

"Shoot!" Sue rubbed shampoo into the Lab's coat and began massaging it into a thick lather. "Guess we'll have to wait 'til she gets back to ask her about that house-keeper. How about the work out there?"

"Suspended until Barry comes back. They both went, some kind of family emergency. I don't know any more than that."

I reached in my pocket, glancing around to make doubly sure we were alone. "But maybe we don't have to wait."

I dangled the key in front of her face.

I thought Sue's eyes were about to pop out of her head. Her expression was so comical, I let out a little giggle before stashing the key back in my pocket.

"Is that . . . ?"

I nodded. "The key to the Tepper house. I took it from the office while Angie wasn't looking. With any luck, no one will miss it, or they'll think Barry has it with him." I shrugged. "I just thought you might want to help me do a little searching tonight."

Sue just stared. Her mouth opened and closed, but no sound came out. For once, she was speechless.

"I'll call you this afternoon," I said, heading for the door. "We can make plans then. Right now, I have to go dig a moat."

It all seemed like a good idea at the time.

A few hours later, parked in Sue's SUV a few doors down from the Tepper house, we weren't so sure. We'd taken Sue's car because it didn't stand out quite as much as either of mine, though the dog barrier across the back-seat was distinctive. Not as much as a candy apple red 'Vette, though.

Sue often used it to pick up or deliver her canine clients, and it smelled of the many dogs who had been passengers.

We sat in the dark, neither one of us ready to leave the relative security of the car and venture down the street to Martha Tepper's house. But neither one of us was ready to call off our adventure, either. We were like a couple of twelve-year-olds who had dared each other into something foolish, and neither one could back down.

"Well, if we're going to do this . . ." I said.

"Then we better get going," Sue finished for me.

It was nearly midnight, the night pitch-black outside the dim glow of a streetlight on the next block. Without consulting each other, we had each shown up dressed all in black, down to the dark sneakers I had fished out of the back of my closet.

I opened my door and slipped out, quickly closing it to extinguish the interior light. Sue did the same. We stood next to the car, waiting for our eyes to adjust.

Key in hand, I led the way down the shoulder of the road to Martha Tepper's driveway. The porch light was out and I had to move slowly, peering into the dark for the cracked concrete walk that led to the front door.

I felt for the lock, and slid the key in.

"Wait here," I whispered to Sue as I locked the door behind us. "Let me check that the drapes are closed before we turn on any lights."

Using the narrow beam of my keychain flashlight, I made my way into the living room, which faced the street. The heavy velvet draperies were open slightly.

I picked my way around the crowded room, narrowly avoiding a collision with an ottoman, and tugged the drapes tightly closed. I checked the other windows, reassuring myself that they were securely covered, then retraced my steps until I reached the entryway, where Sue waited.

I flipped the switch, and the light went on in the hallway. I could see the closed doors to the two bedrooms and the bathroom down the hall to the right, and the kitchen door straight ahead. To the left, the living room was still in shadow, though I could at least make out the shapes of the furniture.

Sue and I glanced at each other. Now that we were here, I wasn't really sure what we were looking for. From the expression on Sue's face, I guessed she wasn't, either.

"Where should we start?" I peered down the hall toward the bedrooms, hesitant to disturb either of them. If we searched Martha Tepper's bedroom, there were only two options. One, we were invading her private, personal space. Or two, she was never coming back to be upset about it.

Neither option was to my liking.

"Let's start in the kitchen," Sue suggested. "If she has any household records, they might be in there."

Sounded like Sue didn't want to touch the bedrooms, either.

It was as good an idea as any, and I pointed toward the kitchen door. "Let's go."

The cabinets looked old enough to have been the originals, and they were badly in need of attention. Drawers stuck and latches didn't. Several cabinet doors drooped open an inch or two. Sue started on the cupboards, and I took the drawers.

I found silverware, spatulas, ladles, and an assortment of inexpensive paring knives. Nothing particularly valuable, or interesting. Another bank of drawers held kitchen linens: dishtowels, pot holders, and several old-fashioned aprons.

No papers. No notes. No clues.

Sue also turned up empty-handed. The cupboards contained only the usual kitchen clutter of plates and cups, pots and pans. There was a pantry in the utility area—the place Barry had called the service porch—but we saved it for later.

We turned off the light and moved into the dining room, where there was a built-in china cabinet with glass-fronted cupboards and deep drawers, filling one entire wall.

There was an uncovered window in the dining room, so we worked by the light of keychain flashlights, shielding the narrow beam of light with our bodies.

The glass-fronted cupboards were easy. They contained Martha Tepper's prized teacup collection, each cup and saucer displayed on a small metal stand. Other than the teacups, the shelves were empty.

I crouched down, pulling open the bottom drawer as Sue peered into the top one. "Table linens," she whispered. She scrabbled through the drawer, checking beneath the top layer. "Tablecloths, hot pads, napkins. That's it." She slid the drawer closed and reached for the next one.

The sound of tires on gravel froze our movements. I released my flashlight, extinguishing the tiny beam of light. A car door closed, the noise like an explosion in the silence.

Footsteps crunched in the gravel, then scuffed along the concrete walkway.

Someone was walking up to the front door!

My heart raced, and I felt the jolt of adrenaline surge through me.

I slid the drawer shut with a trembling hand, praying the scrape of the wooden runners didn't carry outside.

If we were caught in the house, I had planned to say I was looking for a jacket I'd left there while I was working.

It sounded pretty lame, even to me, when I had tried it out on Sue, but it was all we had. And it didn't explain why we were skulking around in the dark, dressed like a pair of overaged ninja wannabes.

Fight or flight? Flight definitely won this time.

A second car pulled up, and we heard another door, and then a voice. We couldn't hear the words or recognize the voice, just the tone, a friendly greeting to the person at the door.

"Come on!" I hissed, grabbing Sue's sleeve.

I pulled her out of the dining room and back into the kitchen. The kitchen door was closed, but we had left the light on in the hallway.

Too late now.

I took a deep breath, and tugged on Sue's sleeve to guide her.

I stepped into the kitchen, reaching out with my left hand to touch the counter. For a moment, all I felt was empty space, and my stomach did a flip, landing somewhere high in my throat.

Then I found the counter's edge, felt the thin metal railing that edged the aging vinyl countertop.

I kept hold of Sue's sleeve with my right hand. I had been in the house several times in the last couple weeks, and Sue was depending on me to get her out safely.

I had to get this right.

The voices outside were fainter through the closed kitchen door, but loud enough for us to know they were still there.

We crept silently across the kitchen. I stuck my foot out with each tiny step, testing the floor ahead of me for any obstruction.

At last we reached the entrance to the service porch.

I twisted the knob slowly as I eased the door open and pulled Sue onto the porch. I turned back and carefully closed the door. The latch slid silently into place.

The moon had risen, its pale light seeping through the screened walls of the service porch. It had probably once been an actual porch, judging from what I had seen of it before. The walls were simple framing, exposed on the inside, with a sheathing of planks covering the outside.

A screen door with a hook led to a set of rough wooden steps down into the backyard.

We made it to the door, and I fumbled with the hook. It finally unlatched, and I pushed the door open, the steps below little more than vague shapes in the faint moonlight.

From inside the house, I heard another door open, and the voices were suddenly louder. I couldn't tell for sure, but I thought at least one voice was male, maybe both.

I pulled Sue in front of me, and gave her a tiny push toward the stairs. This was my idea, and if anyone was going to be caught, it was me.

I heard one of the voices, irritation plain in his tone, say something about leaving the lights on.

Sue was down the steps, and I didn't hang around to hear any more. Whatever was going on inside, I wanted badly to be outside, and away from whoever was in there.

I hung on to the door as I descended the three steps, then carefully closed it. The hook was unfastened, but I could only hope no one would notice, or if they did, they would blame it on careless workmen.

Which would be me. But I'd rather be in trouble for leaving the door unlatched on the job than get caught breaking and entering.

Sue and I faded into the shadows at the side of the yard, slipping between the arbor vitae that formed a gap-toothed hedge between Martha Tepper's house and her neighbors.

We crouched there, barely daring to breathe. Lights went on and off in the kitchen and dining room, and I heard the porch door open and close. But no one checked the screen on the porch, and nobody came out into the yard.

We waited for what seemed like several hours, not daring to move, until we heard a car engine start up and the crunch of tires on gravel as it pulled away.

One down, one to go.

My heart was pounding so hard, I was sure whoever was in the house could hear it.

A block over, a dog barked and another answered, then fell silent. Panic shot through me.

Did Miss Tepper's neighbors have a dog? What if he came out and found us lurking just outside his yard? Would he bark, and give us away?

And why didn't I think about that before I started on

my burglary career? Clearly, I wasn't suited for a life of crime.

Minutes dragged by. My legs cramped from crouching, but I was afraid to move.

Finally, just when I thought my legs would give out, I heard a car door slam and an engine roar to life.

Tires crunched on the gravel driveway, and headlights swept across the front of the house, but didn't pierce the deep shadows in the backyard.

I listened to the dwindling sound of the engine until it faded away, and the neighborhood was quiet once more.

"I think he's gone." Sue's whisper sent my heart racing again, and I bit back a scream.

I waited a moment, quelling the panic that threatened to overwhelm me. "Yeah," I finally managed. "I think so."

I took a deep breath and swallowed again, willing my voice to work properly. "Let's go home."

I took the hint of movement next to me to be a nod of agreement.

Stepping out of the deep shadows took all my resolve. All I wanted to do was cower in the dark. But eventually the sun would come up, and then someone was sure to see us. Waiting didn't seem like a good long-term solution.

I clutched the sleeve of Sue's dark sweatshirt, and we inched our way out into the yard. No dogs barked, no one yelled, and we walked quickly across the open lawn to the far side of the house.

A concrete path led down the side of the house to the street. Tree roots had grown up under the concrete, making the footing dangerous. Sue tripped over a break in the path, but she grabbed my arm and managed to keep her balance.

We reached the front of the house and hurried through the ankle-high grass to the road.

Sue's SUV had never looked so good. The familiar shape loomed darkly in the faint moonlight, its bulk a reassuring presence.

We were a few feet from the car when Sue thumbed the remote, unlocking the doors and lighting the interior.

A man leaned against the car, waiting for us, his silhouette revealed against the interior lights.

This time, I did scream.

He chuckled, and pushed himself away from the car.

"Burglars," Wade said drily, "shouldn't scream. It attracts attention."

I tried to speak, but my vocal cords seemed to have shorted out after that single scream. I opened my mouth. My tongue wouldn't budge, and no sound came out.

Sue recovered first.

"What burglars?" she demanded. She believed the best defense was a good offense, and she was on the offensive.

"Well, what are you two doing here, slinking around in the dark, dressed all in black?"

He had a point, though I wasn't going to admit it.

"Are you the fashion police now?" Sue challenged. "Is there some law against dressing in black?"

Wade chuckled again. He was amused at our predicament. "No fashion crime, ladies. A little trespassing, possibly. But I am sure Georgie has a good explanation, don't you?"

I was grateful that the car lights had faded, so Wade couldn't see me. I could feel a flush of embarrassment rising to my face, hot enough I thought I might glow in the dark.

"Georgie?" Wade's voice turned serious, and he reached out to touch my arm. "I don't know what kind of game you're playing here, but you really could get arrested, you know."

I stiffened, and he gripped my arm tighter. "I'm not going to turn you in or anything," he said. "But you're taking some pretty big chances, and for what?"

"It's a long story," Sue blurted out, "and you won't believe it anyway."

"Try me."

"It's late, Wade." The adrenaline rush had faded and I

was suddenly exhausted. I moved past Wade, his hand still gripping my arm, and sagged against the car. "Can't this wait until the morning?"

Wade released my arm, pushed up his sleeve, and punched a button on his watch. A green glow momentarily lit his features, and I saw a flicker of surprise before the light winked out.

"It is late," he conceded. "Later than I realized.

"Okay. Tomorrow then. I'll pick you up for dinner at six, and I want to hear the whole, long story."

Sue moved to the driver's side of the SUV and opened the door.

"That goes for you, too, Gibbons," Wade added. "I'd love to hear your side of this."

Sue glared at him. "Just what the hell are you doing out here at this hour of the night anyway, Wade?"

"I live here," he answered. "Bought a house right down the street, just last year.

"Martha Tepper and I are neighbors."

chapter 14

"Did you know he'd bought a house?" I asked Sue as we pulled into my driveway.

"Nope." She shook her head. "Told you he moped."

"What?"

She shut off the engine, and turned to face me. "Look, we both need some sleep, but we better figure out what we are going to tell your boyfriend tomorrow night. And I don't think we ought to try that lame story about a missing jacket."

"He is not my boyfriend," I said.

"He didn't rat you out, did he? He acted like he knew you were in that house, and said he wasn't going to turn you in. You don't do that for just anybody, Georgie. He's still carrying that torch, I swear."

"Old friends." It didn't sound convincing, even to me, but I let it drop. "I say we tell him the truth, more or less. I had a key, we were suspicious about Martha Tepper's disappearance, and we went out there to look for clues as to where she went."

Sue shrugged. "A little sugarcoated, but close enough

for me." She started the engine. "Go get some sleep. I'll meet you here as soon as I close up the shop tomorrow."

I nodded and opened the door. "Let's plan to eat here, so we don't have to have this conversation in public. I'll figure something out, and we'll just tell Wade when he gets here."

At twenty minutes to six I stood in the kitchen, staring into the refrigerator. Staring was about all I could do. It was still a bachelor refrigerator: a few microbrews, some leftover faux-Chinese takeout from the supermarket, butter, mayonnaise, and a brick of cheddar cheese, the edges hard and dry from exposure to the air. Should have wrapped that cheese a little better.

The cupboards weren't much better. The sourdough from Katie's had turned dry and hard as a brick. I knew better than to buy two loaves. I hadn't even cut into it.

I was about to surrender to the temptation of Garibaldi's when Sue knocked on the front door.

"Come in," I called. "And help me figure out dinner."

The tapping of stiletto heels on the living room floor told me it wasn't Sue. Not by a long shot.

"I thought you said to come in," my mother said from the kitchen doorway.

I stifled a groan.

"Mom, I have to go to the grocery store. Now. Wade is due for dinner in twenty minutes, and there is nothing here to cook."

"Nonsense," Mom said. She tap-tap-tapped her way across the linoleum to peer into the refrigerator. I tried not to think about the damage those spikes might be doing to my already-worn-out floor. It was Mom's turn to groan. "This isn't a refrigerator, it's a . . . a beer cooler." She pulled out the empty vegetable bins and peered at the egg trays that held only a few individual mustard packets from some long-forgotten fast-food meal.

"Is this how you eat, Georgiana? I taught you better nutrition than this."

She moved away from the refrigerator and began pawing through the cupboards. It took only about ninety seconds to inventory the meager supplies.

She turned back to look at me, her eyes narrowed in thought. "You have an electric skillet, don't you?"

I nodded and opened the bottom cupboard near the sink. The electric frying pan had been a housewarming gift from my mother. I had never used it, but at least I had washed it and removed the tags before I put it away.

"Get a big saucepan out, too," she said. "And a baking sheet." She pulled my meager spice supply from the cupboard. "Where are your knives?"

I gestured to a drawer next to the stove. She tsk-tsked as she looked in the drawer. "You know knives should be stored in a block, Georgiana. They will keep a better edge."

As little as I used my knives—the pizza cutter was my usual tool—it likely didn't make much difference.

Following Mom's direction, I put the skillet on the table.

"Don't turn it on yet, though. You're just going to use it to keep the fondue warm."

"Fondue? Doesn't that take wine and fancy cheese and a special pot and things?"

Mom shook her head. She was already working on cutting up the stale loaf of sourdough, making uniform cubes. "I haven't cooked fondue since your father was in grad school," she said, "but I think I remember how to do it. It won't be the most elegant company meal"—there was a trace of disapproval in her tone, but she didn't belabor the point—"but it should do nicely."

She pointed at the brick of cheddar sitting on the counter next to her. "You need to grate that."

While I grated the cheese, she toasted the bread cubes in the oven and emptied a bottle of microbrew into the saucepan. As the beer heated, she added some garlic powder—"It's better with fresh, but you use what you have"—and a pinch of salt. By the time I'd finished with the cheese, the beer was hot.

Mom handed me a clean plastic trash can bag, with a little flour, salt, and pepper in it. "Put the cheese in there, and shake it, so it gets covered with flour." She gave the bag one last look and stifled a sigh. Obviously I didn't have a proper bag, though she didn't say so.

Soon I was stirring the cheese into the beer, while Mom arranged the bread cubes on plates and heated the electric skillet. She dug around in my junk drawer and dragged out a bag of bamboo skewers. "Use these instead of fondue forks," she said, placing them next to the plates of bread cubes.

She stood back and admired her handiwork. I had to admit, the kitchen smelled pretty darn good. There were placemats on the table, and my good dishes, along with glasses for the iced tea Mom had just made.

"How did you do all that so fast?" I asked. It had been a long time since I'd seen Mom in action, and I had forgotten how good she was at this kind of thing.

"Practice. You just keep doing it, and it comes faster, like any skill. Besides"—she smiled at me—"I couldn't have Wade thinking the only thing you knew how to cook was take-and-bake pizza."

A guilty flush spread over my face and Mom laughed.

"Well, thanks. I guess I owe you one for this."

"It's what any mother would do for her only daughter, and her only daughter's beau." She glanced at her watch, a delicate gold and diamond number. "Speaking of Wade, I better skedaddle before he gets here. Three's a crowd, don't you know?"

I glanced at the gently bubbling pot, and back at Mom.

"Don't walk me to the door," she said. "You need to keep stirring that until it's completely melted. Then put it in the skillet at two hundred degrees to keep it warm while you eat."

"Mom," I said as she headed for the front door, "what did you stop by for, anyway?"

"Nothing important," she called back. "It can wait. You have more important things to worry about tonight."

Fortunately, she was gone before Sue showed up. I don't think her version of my evening included my best friend.

When Sue arrived, I put her to work adding a third setting to the table. She nodded her approval, and waved a grocery bag in front of me.

"I took a chance that you might figure out something, but I was willing to bet it wouldn't include a salad." She took out a packaged Caesar salad, found a bowl in the cupboard, and added the dressing and croutons. She was sprinkling the cellophane envelope of grated parmesan on top when Wade knocked.

"I thought this might be a little more comfortable if we ate here," I said, leading him into the kitchen.

Wade gave a low whistle of appreciation when he saw the table. He sniffed the aromas of cheese, toasted bread, and an undertone of dark ale, and shot me a look of surprise.

"You cooked?"

"I had a little help," I admitted. "But yeah. Didn't you think I knew how?"

The fondue was delicious, and the crisp salad and cold tea were nice contrasts to the hot, gooey cheese.

We made small talk as we ate, but I could feel the tension knotting in my stomach. Soon, Wade would want an explanation for what Sue and I were doing the night before.

The fondue was reduced to a crust around the edge of the pan, and the salad was gone. I unplugged the skillet and put it on the counter to cool.

"Now then," Wade said, "you two owe me a story. And it better be a good one."

I hesitated, feeling the knot in my stomach twist and tighten. I had to tell him.

"I, that is, we . . . we were worried about Miss Tepper. Nobody knows where she is, and I can't get a straight answer out of anybody. Rick Gladstone promised me a forwarding address, but he hasn't called. I had a key to the house, and so we went out to see if we could find some clue as to where she went. An address or a flyer or something from the place she's moving to. Something like that. We figured there had to be something in the house."

Wade snorted. "Dressed all in black, in the middle of the night? With all the lights off? You were just innocently looking for an address? Oh, please!"

"It's the truth," Sue said. "We *are* worried. You can turn us in to whoever it is that you think cares, but we were just trying to find out where she went."

Wade bristled, and glowered at both of us. "Did it look like I was going to 'turn you in' to anyone?" he asked. "Or did I wait, and give you a chance to explain?"

His gaze moved to me, looking deep into my eyes. "I don't want to see you get in trouble. Either of you," he said, glancing over to Sue, then returning to me. "If anyone caught you in that house, with or without a key—which, you will notice I have specifically not asked how you got—you could be in serious trouble."

I colored at the mention of the key. He knew I didn't have any right to have the key, and he didn't want me to try and lie about it.

"Wade," I said, my voice catching in my throat. "I know this looks kinda bad, but there really is a good reason."

He leaned back and crossed his arms, looking at me expectantly. "I'd like to hear it."

"I think something happened to Miss Tepper. I don't think it was her idea to leave, and I don't think she's coming back.

"Ever."

Wade threw his arms in the air and rolled his eyes toward the ceiling. "All because of some sad story Paula Ciccone told you? I warned you about her stories! She dramatizes everything."

"It isn't just that." By now I was practically begging. I wanted Wade to believe me; I needed someone besides Sue to share my fears.

"There's the housekeeper," Sue said. "She lived in the house, and when Miss Tepper moved, she lost her job and her home at the same time."

I cut in, explaining about all the un-Miss-Tepper-like behavior, and our suspicions. Wade let me talk, though I could see it wasn't changing his mind.

Finally, as I ran down, he shook his head. "I don't buy it, Georgie. Martha Tepper was a nice old lady, sure. But she was tired of the cold and the wet, and she had more than earned the right to live where she pleased. She didn't owe anyone in this town a thing.

"In fact, this town owed her. Not that she would think that way, but we all knew she did a lot for the community, even if she kept it quiet. Did you know she funded the first Homes for Help project?"

I shook my head. "That's my point exactly. She had the money to do what she wanted. There are people who would benefit a lot if she went away and never came back," I argued, not ready to give up.

"Like who?" he shot back.

"Like Gregory Whitlock. He's going to make a bundle off that house, and even more off of developing the warehouse site, and you know it."

"And there's the housekeeper, Janis," Sue added. "If Miss Tepper was deserting her, she might have felt she had nothing to lose. Desperation and anger are a bad combination."

"I can't believe you two." Wade shook his head, and shrugged. "Look, I know I'm not going to stop you. You two are determined to keep up your so-called investigation, no matter what I say. So go to it. Have fun."

He reached for my hand, and looked in my eyes. "But I need a favor from you, Georgie. Please."

I didn't answer. I wasn't about to promise anything until I heard what it was he wanted.

"Could you confine your snooping to daylight hours? To times that you might actually have a legitimate reason to be in that house?"

Wade grinned at me, lightening the tension in the room. At least he wasn't threatening to tell anyone about our adventure.

"I suppose," I said. I looked at Sue, and she nodded.

"Thanks." Wade squeezed my hand and winked at me. "It would be darned difficult for me to explain to the rest of the Council if my girlfriend was arrested for breaking and entering. Especially if they found out I knew about it."

At the word *girlfriend*, Sue's eyebrows shot up, and her expression said, "I told you so."

I ignored Sue's gloating, and grinned at Wade. "Girlfriend? Isn't that a bit presumptuous?"

"Maybe," he teased back. "But it could happen. And a cat burglar just doesn't fit with the rising young politician image, now does it?"

I frowned. "You mean this all has to do with your political image?" I pulled my hand away. "Is that it?"

"N-n-no, not at all," Wade stuttered. "I mean, it was just a joke. I was teasing. I didn't mean—"

Sue couldn't keep a straight face any longer, despite my warning glance. She laughed out loud at Wade's predicament.

"Forgot she was the star of the senior play, didn't you?" she said between giggles. "She had you going!"

Wade looked at me. I smiled and spread my arms in a "caught me" gesture.

"Next time we have dinner," Wade muttered, "we are not including your partner in crime."

chapter 15

The problem with "borrowing" something, I realized,
was that you had to return it without getting caught. I'd
been lucky once, when Angie was distracted.

This time was proving a bit more difficult.

I stood near the schedule board, my left hand shoved in
the pocket of my jeans where I clutched the key. Angie
had decided she wanted to be more than just a receptionist, and she had been asking questions about my job for
nearly ten minutes.

I answered in sound bites, designed more for brevity
than clarity, and silently prayed for the phone to ring.
I was back working the McComb site with Sean—Barry
was still gone—and I had to leave soon.

Sean and I had reached a wary truce over the last couple days. I did my job and more, showed up on time, and
kept my mouth shut. More than he could say for most of
the men on the site, and he knew it.

"Are the classes really hard?" Angie asked. That was
her biggest concern, was it "too hard" for her.

"No, as long as you're committed to doing your best," I answered.

"But you're still going to school! Even though you already went to college, and you have a job, and everything!"

"It takes four years, Angie. You take the classes, then you get an apprenticeship while you take more classes, and you take tests to be sure you know what you're doing. That's what all the guys did, and that's what I have to do."

I moved a step closer to the key hooks, waiting for my chance. If nothing happened in another couple minutes, I would have to give up and try tomorrow.

If Barry didn't show up in the meantime, and miss the key.

The phone rang, and I breathed a sigh of relief.

I pulled the key out the instant her back was turned, and reached for the hook. Behind me, I heard Angie bang the phone down, with a curse.

"Salesmen!" she said. "They just—you found it!" Her voice rose at least an octave, the shriek threatening my eardrums.

"You have totally saved my life, I swear." She was practically babbling, relief clear in her expression.

"That key has been missing since Barry left, and I was so afraid it was lost! I mean, at first I thought maybe he took it with him, but he would never do that, and then I was pretty sure I had seen it after he left, anyway. But the hook was empty, and I just knew Barry was gonna be so pissed when he found out I lost it, and—"

Angie stopped to draw a long shuddering breath, and I took advantage of the interruption. "It was right there on the floor." I waved vaguely at the gray, industrial-grade carpet. "Maybe a little under the edge of that bookcase, I think."

I hooked the Tepper key in place, and fished the Beetle key from my other pocket. "Glad to help, but I gotta go. Don't want to be late getting to the site."

I was halfway to the McComb site when the shakes hit

me. I seriously was not cut out for a life of crime. Just getting that key back on its hook was too much stress.

Not to mention the guilt. Not over taking the key, but the upset and worry I caused Angie. There was fallout from my actions that I hadn't even considered, and I wasn't liking it.

Not that I was going to give up my search for clues. But I would change my tactics a little. I would have to be patient until Barry came back, and I had a reason to be in the house.

In the meantime, I hadn't promised not to look around the warehouse. Besides, it wasn't in a residential area, where I was going to be noticed.

At least, that's what I thought.

But when I just happened to drive past the warehouse after work, there were tape and stakes dotting the unpaved parking area. Spray-painted markings showed where various utility lines ran in and out of the building.

Gregory and Sandra were moving ahead with their development plans at the warehouse site. That answered the question about whether Gregory would benefit from Martha Tepper's leaving.

Of course he would. And quickly, if the work at the site was any indication.

I was leery of visiting the warehouse in the dark, and there was too much activity during the day.

Fortunately for my impatience, Barry and Paula returned that evening. Barry called to tell me we were back to work on the Tepper house the next day.

I asked about his trip, and he answered, "Crisis averted," in a relieved tone.

"I imagine you'll be glad to give up digging that moat," he continued with a chuckle.

"It's not so bad," I answered. "I think Sean has decided I'm not completely useless. But I'll be glad to get back to work on the house so Sandra will stop calling three times a day, asking when we'll be through."

Barry's tone grew serious. "Tell her to call me, Georgie. She needs to remember the chain of command around here. Your job assignments, and all the other schedule issues, are my problem, not yours.

"She may be your mother, but I'm still the boss.

"Just don't repeat that to Paula."

I laughed. "I won't, but now that you mention it, I do need to talk to her. Is she there?"

Barry turned the phone over to Paula, and we arranged to meet after work the next day.

"Come on, guys," I called to the dogs after I hung up. "We all need some exercise."

And I needed to think. I locked the door behind us, tugging at the knob to make sure it was secure, and headed out.

Spring was giving way to summer, daylight lingering later each day. The weather still held a cool dampness, but there was a promise of warmer weather to come.

Pine Ridge often had a few dry weeks in the height of summer, but for most of the year it still held a hint of the rain and snow that gave the Great North-wet its nickname.

We walked along the shoulder, Daisy and Buddha exploring the damp grass and salal thickets along the side of the road as I considered what I knew about Martha Tepper's disappearance.

We were just a block from Main Street. On impulse, I tugged the dogs toward the closed shops that made up the commercial center of Pine Ridge.

I found myself standing in front of the empty storefront, peering through the gaps in the brown paper taped over the windows.

I wondered if Pine Ridge could support a dojo. Not that I had any money to spend, or any idea what to do, but I knew I couldn't be the only one in town who could use a little stress relief.

When I reached the Tepper house the next morning, I was surprised to see Sean's battered pickup truck parked behind Barry's behemoth.

Barry greeted me at the door. "Good to see you again, Georgie." I suppressed a grin. Even on the work site, he couldn't break the habit of holding doors.

"Sean's here for a couple days," he continued, leading me through the house to the kitchen. "The McComb site is shut down again; more permit issues. They're going to end up spending as much on lawyers and permits as they pay us to build the blasted thing."

I followed him into the kitchen. Sean stood waiting, three steaming cups of coffee on the counter next to him. He didn't actually smile—but at least he didn't growl—as he handed me a cup. "Morning, Neverall," he said.

I nodded back at him, took the cup, and said, "Thanks."

Barry motioned to the stained and chipped kitchen sink. "This is going," he said between sips of the scalding coffee. "We need to replace the feed lines and the valves, and get it ready for the new sink and faucets.

"The moving crew is supposed to clear this place day after tomorrow, and then we'll be able to work in the basement. There are a couple places where they replaced galvanized pipe with copper, and there's some serious problems at the joints."

I nodded my understanding. Galvanized pipe and copper pipe did not play well together. If they were directly connected, galvanic corrosion would eat away at the steel pipe. I allowed myself a moment of self-congratulation for remembering the classroom lesson, then turned my attention to the problem at hand: how to look for clues with both Sean and Barry around.

And Barry had just said the movers would be taking everything away in two days, so I had to work fast, if I was going to find anything before it all disappeared.

Barry assigned Sean to the bathroom, since he could work alone. Barry and I would tackle the kitchen.

I wrestled with the shut-off valves under the kitchen sink for several minutes, without success. They were in worse shape than the bathroom valves, and I finally admitted defeat, sliding out from the cramped undersink cabinet.

"Sorry, Barry. I can't get those suckers to budge. Maybe we should just shut off the water at the street."

Barry, however, had a large dose of stubborn, and was not about to give up. He grabbed a long-handled wrench for more leverage, and wiggled into the tight space under the sink.

He grunted and groaned as he tried to close the valves, finally asking for a shorter wrench. There wasn't room to use the long wrench he had initially chosen.

As he struggled with the wrench, I glanced around the kitchen. Sue and I had searched it before, but we could have missed something. I slipped off my heavy work gloves and opened cupboard doors and pulled out drawers, confirming our fruitless search of a few days earlier.

"What are you doing up there?" Barry's muffled voice came from under the sink, followed by a grunt of effort.

"Nothing," I answered, trying to close the drawer I had opened without making any more noise.

"Well, how about going out to the street and finding the shutoff?" Barry said.

I smiled as I went out the door. He hadn't actually said to turn the water off—that would be admitting defeat, after all—but I knew that was what he expected me to do.

Easier said than done. The front yard had benefited from the soft spring rain, and I guessed it hadn't been cut since Miss Tepper left. I tromped through the thick, ankle-high grass, and dug beneath the fresh foliage of the bushes that defined the property line, looking for the shutoff.

I finally found the concrete cover a few feet west of the mailbox, obscured by the grass and a stand of calla lilies that had spread around the concrete vault that held the valve.

I passed Barry coming out of the house as I was going back in. "Need to check the truck for replacement parts," he said. "Back in a minute."

I took advantage of the time, hurrying to the dining room. I wanted a chance to look in the drawers of the built-in china hutch, where Sue and I had been interrupted on our previous visit.

I opened the bottom drawer, which I hadn't had time to search before, and peered inside. It looked empty, but there was a scrap of paper, caught in the back of the drawer, as though a corner had ripped off something larger.

I grabbed the piece, but it was stuck between the back of the drawer and the bottom of the drawer above. At least I understood how it had ripped off. I tugged, but it didn't move.

I heard Barry open the front door. I had only a few seconds. Taking the drawer pull in my other hand, I wiggled the drawer while pulling gently on the scrap. It slid free, and I stuffed it in my pocket.

I pushed the drawer shut, praying it wouldn't make noise, and walked back into the kitchen a couple seconds before Barry returned.

He looked disgusted. "I was afraid of this. It's an old house, and I don't have the right size replacement on the truck."

He pulled out his cell phone and hit the speed dial. His suppliers were all on speed dial. He talked for a minute with Frank at All-Ways, then flipped the phone closed.

"Frank has the valves, but no one to deliver them today. I'm going to go pick them up, and you can help Sean with the bathroom while I'm gone."

Not what I wanted to hear, but at least I got to stay in the house. Maybe I could look around a little more.

"I'll tell Sean," he said, heading down the hall.

I looked longingly at the china hutch, tempted to look in one more drawer before following him down the hall.

But he was already curious, and I didn't want to arouse any suspicion.

Barry roared off in his truck and I was left with Sean, and a bathroom that needed the fixtures removed.

"Let's do this, Neverall." Sean nodded at the toilet. "This has got to go before the floor guys can come in."

Sean already had the supply lines disconnected. He motioned to the tank. "You want to get the tank bolts?"

It wasn't really a question. Besides, there wasn't much room around the toilet, and I was a lot smaller than Sean.

I pulled on my gloves, crouched down next to the tank, and fitted a wrench to the nut under the ledge of the toilet. Sean reached inside the empty tank and immobilized the bolt. I pushed hard against the wrench handle, but the nut didn't budge. I pushed again, without result.

Above me, I thought I heard a self-satisfied "Um-hmm" from Sean. I was proving his point that women were unfit for this work, and I wasn't going to give him that satisfaction. I concentrated on the wrench and the nut, focusing my energy.

I pushed again, beads of sweat popping out of my forehead and running toward my eyes. I kept up the pressure, my arms straining with the effort.

Metal screeched against metal, accumulated years of corrosion grinding in the threads of the nut, but it moved slightly.

I instantly reset the wrench, and put all my effort into it. The nut moved, easier this time. A couple more pushes, and it twisted easily off the bolt.

As I stood up to move to the other side, I forced myself to keep a straight face when I glanced at Sean. He was doing the same, and we nodded curtly as we positioned ourselves to extract the other bolt.

We repeated the procedure on the other side, and we soon had the tank loose from the bowl. Now we had to lift off the tank and take it outside.

There wasn't room for both of us, so I waved Sean

aside. Tanks are heavy, a job for two people whenever possible. But it wasn't possible, and I was determined to prove myself.

I got a grip on the tank, bracing myself for the lift, and carefully raised the tank straight up a few inches. With the seat already off, that was all that I needed.

The empty tank was still heavy, and I felt the strain in my back and down my legs, but I wasn't going to admit it to Sean.

I turned toward the door, the tank clutched against my chest. Sean backed away, clearing the way for me.

The tank shifted in my arms, and I hugged it tighter.

There was an ominous cracking noise, and the tank slipped a little more.

I tried to shift the weight, to tighten my hold.

It moved again, with a noise like rocks slamming against each other, and to my horror the bottom fell out.

The heavy slab of porcelain slammed against my ankle and I stumbled, bashing my shin against the side of the bathtub.

Sean rushed forward, grabbing the remains of the tank from me. The bottom had landed on my boot and I was instantly grateful for the steel cap in the shoe. Without it, my toes would have been crushed by the slab of porcelain.

Adrenaline surging through my veins hollowed my stomach, and sent my heart racing. My knees suddenly refused to support me, and I sank down on the edge of the tub.

Sean returned to the bathroom. Without speaking, he stooped and picked up the bottom of the tank.

By the time he came back, I was on my feet, although I had to lean against the vanity.

Sean's face was pale; the shock of the accident had drained all his color. He stared at me for a minute, as though he didn't know what to say.

"Are you"—his voice was strained, almost a squeak— "okay?"

"I, uh, I think so." I was rather squeaky myself. I stopped to swallow. Hard.

"Can you walk?"

Why would he ask that? I thought for a moment, and realized what he must have seen. The tank broke, a large chunk slammed my left leg and landed on my foot, and I fell onto the edge of the bathtub.

To find the answer to his question, I let go of the vanity and gingerly put a little weight on my injured leg.

My ankle twinged, but it held.

I leaned on the leg, putting more weight on it, and a sharp pain ran up my calf and thigh.

I bit my lip to keep from whimpering, but Sean saw the flash of pain that crossed my face. He reached out, offering me his arm.

"Come on in the dining room," he said. "There are chairs in there, and you can sit down."

I tried to hide my surprise at his change of heart, but I don't think I was very successful. "Don't look so shocked, Neverall. I'd do the same for anyone who got hurt on the job."

I let Sean help me into the dining room, where I lowered myself onto a high-backed wooden chair.

"I'm going to call Barry," Sean said. "My phone's in the truck. You okay for now?"

"Fine, fine," I muttered. To tell the truth, my ankle hurt like hell, and I knew I was going to have a nasty bruise on my foot—and a couple other places, as well.

Sean gave me a look that said he didn't really believe me, but when I didn't say anything more, he shrugged and went out.

Despite the pain in my leg and ankle, I realized I was alone in the dining room. This was my chance to investigate.

I pulled my gloves off and scooted my chair toward the china hutch. There were still two drawers to go.

The drawers were a bust. Nothing except china, silver, and a box of antique silver napkin rings.

The napkin rings looked like family heirlooms, an intricate band of woven strands. On the side of each ring was a medallion engraved with an ornate capital *T*.

Who leaves family heirlooms for some unknown person to pack?

Someone without a choice.

chapter 16

It wasn't a comforting thought.

I didn't have time to follow that path before Sean and Barry both came in the house.

Accidents happen on job sites. It's a fact of life, especially in the construction industry. As accidents go, this was pretty benign. But Barry looked more than worried; he looked angry.

"What happened?"

"I don't know. We got the tank loose and I lifted it off the bowl. It felt, I don't know, slippery. Kept sliding and slipping. Then, boom! The bottom fell out, crashed into my leg and landed on my foot."

Barry turned to Sean. "Have you looked at the tank?"

"Not yet. I helped Georgie in here to sit down, then I went and called you." He shrugged. "You were almost here when I called, so I just waited."

Well, that explained how I had time to check both those drawers; Sean was waiting outside for Barry, rather than coming back in the house with me.

"Can you walk?" Barry asked me. "I want to go get a look at that tank, and I thought you might be curious."

I tried to stand. My ankle throbbed, but at least the stabbing pain was gone this time.

I waved away Barry's offered arm and hobbled to the front door under my own power. I'd taken worse knocks in the early days of my martial arts training, and learned to work through the pain. This wasn't much different.

Sean had dumped the two chunks of porcelain in the high grass of the front yard. The walls of the tank were in a single piece, sitting on its side next to the flat slab that had been the bottom of the tank.

I limped across the grass, my left ankle warning me of worse pain to come. There was no way I could balance on my throbbing ankle to crouch or kneel to examine the pieces closely.

Barry knelt in the tall grass and grasped the tank. He turned it over several times, looking at, and touching, the outside surface before he looked up at me.

"There's something greasy on the back of the tank," he said. "Were you wearing gloves?"

"Yep." Gloves at all times was another Barry rule, a safety precaution I had learned to appreciate. If the porcelain had given way at another point, the sharp edge could have sliced my hands open.

He nodded. "That explains why you didn't feel it." He peered closely at the backside of the tank. "Something must have spilled down the back of the tank, and no one could reach it to clean it up."

Sean stood next to me, looking down at the tank. "How about the bottom, though? How the he—heck"—he caught himself before he broke the cussing rule—"did that happen?"

Barry moved over to the tank bottom, and Sean crouched next to him. The two men examined the slab, occasionally pointing to one spot or another and exchanging grunts.

I was beginning to feel invisible when Barry looked

back up at me. "Looks like there was a crack in the bottom of the tank. When you moved it and released the compression, the crack spread around the perimeter of the tank, and it gave way."

"Just another example," I deadpanned, "of why gravity is not your friend."

Barry chuckled mirthlessly, as he climbed to his feet.

"I think you're done here for today, Georgie. Go get that ankle looked at." He stopped my protest with a gesture. "That's an order, Neverall. On-the-job accidents are reportable, and we need to document any injury." He glanced at his watch. "Dr. Cox should be at the Immediate Care. I'll tell him to expect you."

"Okay." He was worried about me, but he was following the rules, too. Even though I clearly wouldn't make trouble for Barry, it was a rule that could prevent bigger problems, and we all had to abide by it.

I limped over to the Beetle and dropped into the driver's seat. Sean appeared in the door opening, leaning over to look in at me. "Can you handle that clutch?" he asked. "My truck's an automatic, if you want to use it."

"I'm fine," I answered. "But thanks for asking."

"No problem," he replied. "Barry says let him know what the doc says." He patted the roof of the Beetle. "Later."

I waited until he stepped away from the car before putting my hand on the gearshift and pushing down to disengage the clutch. The Beetle's automatic stick shift meant I didn't need a clutch pedal at all, but that would be my little secret.

On a weekday afternoon, the Immediate Care waiting room was nearly empty when I hobbled in. At the counter, the receptionist handed me a stack of forms and asked if I had a referral from my employer.

"No, we were on a job site. Do you need that?"

"It's Hickey & Hickey, right? I can call Angie and have her fax it over." She reached for the stack of papers and took out several pages. "Angie should be able to take care of most of these for you, too."

There were advantages to a small town.

She motioned for me to come around the counter, and showed me to a treatment room in the back. "You can fill out the paperwork here," she said, "so you can get off the foot and stay off it. Dr. Cox should be just a couple minutes."

Dr. Cox had taken over my father's practice a few months after Dad's death, moving it from the outdated office on Main Street into larger quarters and increasing the staff. I didn't know him well, but my mother had given me all the pertinent details. At least, by her standards.

Dr. Cox was a veteran of the Centers for Disease Control, better known as the CDC, but had tired of the climate in Atlanta and the travel, she said. He was looking for a small-town practice, and she was searching for a buyer for Dad's practice. Best of all, she said when the deal was made, Dr. Cox was single.

Before I returned to Pine Ridge, though, he acquired a wife and a new baby, thwarting my mother's matchmaking plans and saving us both a lot of potential embarrassment.

The nurse came in and helped me out of my boots and jeans. She propped my foot up, and offered me a sheet. "The doctor will be with you in just a few minutes," she said, closing the door.

A few minutes were more like fifteen.

"What happened to you, Georgiana?" Dr. Cox asked. He flipped through the notes the nurse had left on the door, then glanced back up at me.

"You dropped a toilet on your ankle?" There was a note of disbelief in his voice.

"Just part of the tank," I answered, then explained how the accident had happened. "Nothing broken, but I'm going to have some exciting bruises, and Barry—Mr. Hickey—insisted on an exam because I was injured on the job."

Thirty minutes later I was back in the car, my ankle wrapped, a few painkillers in my pocket, and instructions to ice the ankle and keep it elevated. The bruises would heal by themselves, though I anticipated some interesting colors in the next few days.

Dr. Cox, like Sean, had asked about the clutch in the Beetle, and I had shared my secret. Hey, doctor-patient confidentiality covered that information, didn't it?

Daisy and Buddha greeted me at the door, both waiting expectantly next to the hook with the leashes.

"Not today, guys. Sorry."

I limped through the house and opened the back door for them. The yard wasn't as good as a walk, but they raced outside and started sniffing the bushes.

While the dogs were exploring the backyard, checking to see if any new smells had appeared since their last visit, I hobbled back into the kitchen.

My message light blinked, and I mashed the button before lowering myself into the office chair in front of what I laughingly referred to as my desk. It was really just a tiny spot of counter with the cabinet doors removed, but it served its purpose.

There was a message from my mother, with a question about the work on the Tepper house. I'd call her later, and tell her to ask Barry.

Paula had called to check on our plans for tonight. Barry had told her about my accident, she said, and maybe we ought to cancel if I wasn't up to it.

I glanced at my watch, then picked up the phone and dialed the library. Paula answered on the second ring.

"I could use the distraction," I told her. "I am stuck in the house with my foot up and an ice pack on it. I'm going to call Sue to help with the dogs, and I'm ordering pizza. You good with pepperoni?"

Sue was my next call. When I told her what had happened, she gasped. "Don't you think that's kind of suspicious?" she asked. "As soon as you start looking around, a toilet falls apart and practically breaks your leg? That's just not the kind of coincidence I believe in."

"Oh, come on! You're starting to sound like one of those old detective shows. It was an accident, and I'm fine. Besides, there was no guarantee I was going to lift that tank."

"Unless Sean was in on it," Sue said ominously. The roller coaster made a sudden dip, and she continued, "I'm on my way. And maybe Paula and I together can convince you this means something."

"We'll see."

I called Barry and filled him in on Dr. Cox's report. "I should be back tomorrow, Bear. The ankle's wrapped, and he says it's just bruised."

I listened patiently as Barry told me to take my time, don't rush it, blah blah blah. Fortunately for me, he couldn't see me rolling my eyes like a moody teenager.

I don't do "rest" well, and my patience was shot. I was counting on Sue and Paula to lighten my mood.

What was I thinking?

Paula was right on time, arriving just a couple minutes before the pizza delivery while Sue was giving the dogs their post-walk treats.

Paula didn't waste any time. Before I even had my first piece of pizza, she said, "Now do you believe me that Martha didn't leave town voluntarily?"

"I know no such thing, Paula."

"She does too," Sue chimed in. "She just doesn't want to admit it. I don't either, for that matter, but this . . ." She waved at my taped-up ankle, resting on a pillow next to the pizza. "This makes me wonder."

I lowered my foot to the floor, out of her line of sight, and reached for a piece of pizza. Sue glared at me. "I could have handed that to you," she said accusingly. "Now get that foot back up."

"Yes, Mom." I leaned back and put my foot back up.

"Seriously." Paula went back to her one-track conversation. "Why else would that tank break just when you picked it up?"

"Uh, because it was cracked?" I sighed with exasperation. "Really, guys. It was an accident. Stuff happens, especially in old houses."

"It wasn't," Paula said quietly.

Sue and I both stared at her. How in the world could she say such a thing? She held my gaze for a silent moment, then continued. "I heard Barry talking to Gregory on the phone. He said it looked like there was a fresh crack in the side of the tank, and he told Gregory he couldn't imagine any way that happened accidentally.

"From what I heard, it sounded like Gregory didn't believe him." Her voice rose in indignation. "Barry would never lie about something like that!"

A chill ran down my back. Barry had told the one person I completely distrusted about my accident.

"Why did it have to be Gregory?"

I didn't realize I had voiced the thought until Sue answered. "Duh! He owns the house, or at least he will as soon as the paperwork gets done. He's responsible if someone gets hurt on the job site."

That argument had some merit, but I still thought Gregory was a prime suspect. "You may be wrong there, Sue. It's a job site; the contractor is responsible for the safety of his employees. It's Barry's responsibility, not Gregory's."

Paula nodded. "That's what Barry kept saying. That he would be the one in trouble for on-the-job injuries. He was upset about Georgie, and he wanted to be sure no one else got hurt." She looked at my ankle and back at me. "Do you really think Gregory might have something to do with this?"

"She hates him," Sue said around a mouthful of pizza. "Hates the idea that her mother is sl—"

A well-aimed sofa pillow interrupted her. I'd always had a pretty good arm, if I say so myself.

"Well, it's true." Sue had the good sense to duck this time, and the other pillow sailed harmlessly past her.

"Now that you're out of ammunition," Paula said to me, "can you answer my question? I'm serious, Georgie.

Do you really think Gregory Whitlock could have anything to do with your accident, and with Martha's disappearance?"

"If not him," I asked, "then who else? I mean, he has the most to gain, doesn't he? If Martha disappears, he can pretty much do anything he wants to that property. She can't stop him from whatever plans he has."

"Except that he could do that anyway, as soon as the sale goes through," Sue said.

"Unless she changed her mind once she found out what he was planning," I replied. "He's going to develop that tract out by the warehouse, and maybe she didn't like the idea. I know he's planning to flip the house, and he expects to make a *lot* of money off it. Maybe she didn't like that plan, either."

"How do you define 'a lot'?" Paula made quote marks in the air with tomato-smeared fingers.

"Neighborhood of low- to mid-six-figure houses, based on what I saw."

Paula's mouth formed a little O.

Sue sucked in a deep breath. "Nice neighborhood."

"That's what I thought. He has several thousand reasons to want her out of the way."

"What about the housekeeper?" Sue asked.

"Janis." I turned to Paula. "That was one of the things I wanted to ask you about. Do you know Miss Tepper's housekeeper?"

Paula looked thoughtful for a moment. "She was angry when Martha left, even came by the library, thinking I knew where she went."

"Can't say as I blame her," Sue said. "Losing your job and your home at the same time, without any warning."

"That's not true! She did have warning." Paula leaped to Miss Tepper's defense. "Martha had been talking about moving for weeks, maybe months, before she left."

"Justified or not," I said, "she was angry. Was she angry enough to do something before Miss Tepper left? Desperate people do desperate things, after all."

"I don't believe it." Paula's mouth was set in a tight line. "Janis loved Martha, would do anything for her. And she thought Martha was coming back to pack and close the house. That was what she asked about when she came to the library.

"Of course that was before Rachel Gladstone threw her out." She grimaced.

Sue shot me a glance, clearly remembering my suspicions of my mother. "Rachel threw her out?" she asked.

Paula nodded her head.

Sue leaned forward, her hands clasped in front of her, anticipating a story.

"The way I heard it from Janis, Rachel showed up in 'that big car,' and told her the house was going to be sold and she had to get out. Janis said she came in the afternoon and wouldn't let her stay that night, or even pack her clothes, or get any of her things.

"She threatened to call the police if Janis didn't leave. The poor thing had to sleep in her car." Her voice shook with indignation, and I was reminded of Wade's warning about Paula's dramatic stories.

"It was probably the buyer's idea." I wasn't ready to let my mother completely off the hook. "I bet they made Rachel evict her, instead of doing it themselves."

"Now that doesn't sound like Sandra Neverall," Sue said. "Your mother is one tough cookie when it comes to her work. She doesn't pass the buck."

"What about Gregory?" I shot back. "And if it isn't them, who is it?"

"Well, what about the Gladstones?" Sue countered. "Rachel apparently was the one who threw Janis out."

Before I could say anything, the phone rang. Sue jumped up to answer it for me, with an expression that looked suspiciously like relief.

She returned, carrying the phone at arm's length, and handed it to me. *Your mother*, she mouthed.

My heart sank. I knew, just from Sue's expression, that I was in trouble. The only question was, how much.

A lot, as it turned out.

"Georgiana? Georgiana, what happened?"

"What do you mean?" I tried to play dumb, as though I didn't know what she was talking about.

"You know perfectly well what I mean." Righteous indignation radiated over the phone line. "Why is it I am the last person in the world to find out that my daughter was practically killed?"

"Why, I'm just fine, actually. Thank you for asking. It's just a couple little bruises. But I do appreciate your concern."

I couldn't keep the sarcasm completely out of my voice, and my mother pounced. "Of course I'm concerned, Georgiana! And it isn't just a couple bruises, according to your boss. He told Gregory you were seriously injured, and he practically accused him of causing the accident!"

"Mother! Calm down. I'm sure Barry didn't say that. He was concerned about the accident, sure. After all, he's responsible for whatever happens on the job site, and it could have been a lot worse than it was.

"But it is just a couple bruises, and I'm going back to work in the morning, so it isn't any big deal."

"Well . . ." Mom sounded unconvinced. "It was very embarrassing, Georgiana. We were having dinner, and Gregory said he hoped you were going to be okay, and I had no idea what he was talking about. You should have called me!"

I sighed. "I probably should have, Mom. It just didn't seem like a big deal."

"All right," she said. "Next time, please let me know, okay? I have to go, Gregory's still at the dinner table, and I'm sure he's wondering what's taking me so long in the kitchen."

She giggled, a sound that sent another chill down my spine. "Okay. Mom? Would you please remind him he was going to get me Martha's forwarding address?" It was just a little dig, but it made me feel better.

Sue took the phone from me with a knowing grin.

"You didn't tell your mom you got hurt, huh? And she heard about it from Gregory?"

I bristled. "Do you call your mother every time you get hurt at work?" I countered.

"When I get hurt at work," Sue called over her shoulder as she carried the phone to the kitchen, "it's a scratch from an overexcited puppy. Not somebody dropping a toilet on me."

"Don't exaggerate! It was just a piece of the tank, and nobody dropped it on me. It was an accident."

"No it wasn't. Paula told you what Barry said."

I glanced at Paula, and she nodded.

"Whatever," I muttered. "Paula, I did have one other question, though. Do you know if Janis had a key to Miss Tepper's house? I mean, she said she waited until 'that woman'—I guess she meant Rachel Gladstone—went away and left the house unlocked. But is it possible she has a key, and she could get back in?"

Paula shook her head. "I don't think so. She said Rachel took her key."

5

♦

prevent collateral damage

Duct tape placed around the jaws of your pliers will help prevent scratches on the polished surfaces of faucets and drains.

—A Plumber's Tip from Georgiana Neverall

chapter 17

Our evening ended on a somber note. Instead of offering some relief from my dark mood, the conversation had reinforced my greatest fear.

We all had the same thought: Martha Tepper had not left Pine Ridge by choice. Something bad had happened to her, and we might never see her again.

Paula's pain was almost physical. When she finally allowed the realization to sink in, she doubled over as though she had taken a shot to the gut.

"We need to tell someone," she said, her voice thick and her eyes glistening with moisture.

"Like who?" Sue asked.

"Can't we file a missing person report with the police?" Paula was desperate for action.

"They'll want some kind of proof." I tried to control the bitterness. I remembered trying to convince some junior detective in San Francisco that Blake Weston and his pals were stealing from Samurai Security. He told me I needed evidence, not just suspicion, and to come back when I had it.

"Then how about your boyfriend?" Paula said.

Despite the serious subject, I saw Sue's mouth twitch at the mention of Wade.

"He's not my boyfriend. He's just someone I've gone out with a couple times."

"He was your boyfriend, wasn't he? And you're dating again. That's got to count for something. Besides, he's on the City Council. Maybe he could get the sheriff to at least search the house or something." Paula was pleading now, anxious for someone, anyone, to take up the hunt for Martha Tepper.

Against my better judgment, I agreed to talk to Wade.

I blame the pain pills.

Wade, of course, didn't take well to the suggestion he help out with our investigation. Even when I cooked dinner. Okay, so it was meatloaf, packaged salad, and baked potatoes, but at least I couldn't mess that up.

It didn't help.

"You want me to do what?" he asked. "That is a bad idea in more ways than I want to think about."

"I didn't think you'd go for it," I confessed.

I stood up and carried the stack of dirty dishes to the counter.

"There are just so many things that don't add up. I hoped maybe you could do something that would help put Paula's mind to rest and answer our questions about Martha."

"Georgie." Wade got up from the table and moved over next to me. He set down the empty salad bowl and took my hands in his. "I know you want to reassure Paula, and that's a fine and generous motive. But I can't order the sheriff's department to open an investigation; and I can't ask them to check into something based on your feelings."

His grip was gentle, and I found myself curling my fingers around his.

"I'm really sorry," he said. "But I don't have any authority here. There isn't anything I *can* do, even if I wanted to. It's the sheriff's job, and Fred Mitchell doesn't welcome interference from anybody. Martha simply moved away. Maybe she didn't plan it as well as she should have, but that's all there is to it."

Wade kept hold of my hand, drawing me away from the sink and into the living room. He pulled me down next to him on the sofa, and turned to look in my eyes.

"But what if she changed her mind? What if she decided not to move after all? Then Gregory Whitlock would lose the chance to develop the warehouse site, and to flip Miss Tepper's house, and maybe even whatever money he'd already put into the project."

Wade shook his head. "Gregory Whitlock didn't get to be one of the most successful businessmen in the area by being stupid. This project isn't big enough to risk his company and his reputation.

"There are people in this town who resent him because he's made a lot of money. There are people who think he's arrogant—even me, sometimes. But he knows where the line is, and while he may dance along it, he's careful not to cross over.

"Do you think I'd accept his support, and his campaign contributions, if there was anything shady going on?"

"Oh." I winced.

"Right. You don't like the guy because he's sleeping—"

"Don't!" I put my fingers in my ears, like an eight-year-old. "La la la . . ."

Wade reached up and pulled my fingers away from my ears. "Sleeping with your mother," he finished his sentence, then looked around the room. "Well, look at that. I said it, and the world did not come to an end. How about that?"

I yanked my hands away.

"I don't want to talk about it, and I don't want to think about it," I said.

I couldn't tell Wade I knew Gregory's type all too well, knew about the sincere looks and the reassuring words. Knew all about trusting someone with your business, and your heart, right up to the point where they destroyed both.

"You don't have to like him, Georgie. Heck, there are times I don't like him much. But he's smart and successful, and he seems to make your mother happy." He shrugged. "Settle for that, for now. It could be worse. I know."

I looked skeptical, and Wade colored. He looked away, then looked back, as though he had come to a decision.

"When my folks split up . . ." He stopped and cleared his throat. "When my dad left," he said. The words were difficult for him, and he paused again.

"My dad left. It wasn't a mutual decision. There was"—he sighed—"another woman. One too young for me to date, much less my dad.

"They left town, and Mom never talked about it. No one knows. But that little—" He bit back a word Barry probably wouldn't have approved of. "That woman made my dad's life miserable—for the year she stayed. Now he's alone, and Mom won't talk to him, so believe me, I know it can be worse."

"Oh, Wade! I am so sorry! I had no idea . . ."

"No one does." He shrugged. "My point is, at least your mom is happy. Be thankful for that."

It was my turn to sigh. "You're right. I'm probably not being fair to Gregory. But can we not talk about my mother, please?"

Wade nodded. "Deal. If we can not talk about Martha Tepper, too."

I stuck out my hand. "Deal."

I stood up. "There are leftovers to put away," I said. "Give me a couple minutes?"

Wade shook his head and stood up, too. "I'll help."

We worked together until the table was clear and the leftovers tucked safely in the refrigerator.

My mother would be proud of me.

When I pulled up in front of the Tepper house the next morning, I was dismayed to see a moving van parked at the curb and planks laid across the tall grass of the front yard.

Three burly men trundled handcarts across the boards, loaded with Miss Tepper's furniture. I watched with a sinking heart as they loaded her highboy waterfall dresser into the van, followed by the matching night tables. The pieces were antiques, and I could only guess at their value. But the men pushing them didn't seem to care, shoving them carelessly into the truck.

Inside, the situation was much worse. Several men in various shapes and sizes haphazardly tossed the contents of cupboards and drawers into cardboard cartons. In each room, one man wielded a black felt-tip marker, scrawling "bedroom," or "living room," or "kitchen" on the box before adding it to a shaky pile in the living room, ready to be carted to the truck.

The men smelled of sweat and stale cigarette smoke, and I remembered Rachel Gladstone telling my mother they had hired a crew from the Second Chances shelter.

I watched from a corner of the living room for several minutes, as they moved furniture and filled boxes. Although they weren't gentle with Martha's things, they all worked hard. The house would be empty soon.

Judging by the raised voices in the kitchen, not everyone was happy about it.

When I peeked around the corner, I wasn't surprised to find my mother in the middle of the disagreement. In the years since my father's death, she had become increasingly confident and self-assured. She had also become a lot more vocal about her opinions.

Rick Gladstone was getting the full force of Sandra the Real Estate Agent's opinions, and he was clearly not enjoying the process.

"You want me to sell this house, don't you? I mean, that *is* why you hired Whitlock Estates, right? You said Martha Tepper told you to 'spruce it up' and sell it, and that's what you told us to do. So let us do our job."

"But the expense," Rick said. His silky voice was gone for the moment, and he just sounded whiny. "This is going to cost us a fortune in labor and storage fees. And now you tell me you don't want the furniture moved back in when the renovations are complete?"

Sandra shook her head firmly. "Damn straight."

I slid back into the hallway, out of sight of the kitchen, and bit my lip. I couldn't remember ever hearing my mother curse, not once. But this was Sandra the Real Estate Agent, not my mother.

I peeked back around the corner. In her ever-present stilettos, my mother was nearly as tall as Gladstone, and her stiff posture made her appear taller. The two of them stood only a few feet apart, though Mom had clearly established a no-man's-land between them.

Rick Gladstone, however, wasn't backing down. "Ms. Neverall." He leaned toward her and controlled the whine, dropping his voice to the silky tone I had heard before. "Sandy—"

For a split second, I really thought Mom might actually deck him. She looked that angry.

"Don't call me that," she said. Her voice was low and cold. "No one calls me that, even my late husband. God rest his soul."

"But I thought, that is . . ." Rick Gladstone tried to cover his confusion with an engaging grin, but it didn't melt Sandra Neverall. I could have told him that. "Isn't that what Greg calls you?"

"What Mr. Whitlock calls me and what you call me are two very different things, Mr. Gladstone. *Gregory*"—she stressed the name, clearly implying that no one called him

Greg any more than they called her Sandy—"is an old and dear friend, and I tolerate it from him. Anything more is none of your business."

Rick Gladstone finally caught a clue, and backed away a step. "I meant no offense, Ms. Neverall. Please accept my apology. I just thought, since we're working together, we might be friends."

He offered the grin again and Sandra thawed about two degrees, from Ice Queen to chilly. It wasn't a vast improvement.

"But seriously," he pressed on. "We could put the furniture back in the house. Make it look like someone actually lives here. More homey."

"We most certainly cannot. I know you want to save the cost of the storage, but frankly, I can't get top dollar for this place with the outdated furniture crowded into these rooms. The place is small to begin with, and with oversized old furniture stuffed into every room . . ." She shook her head. "It would never sell."

She glanced toward the dining room. "It must be family heirlooms. I can't imagine why she didn't take *any* of it with her."

Rick hesitated, and I thought for a minute he wasn't going to respond. Finally he said, "She's staying in temporary quarters. No sense in moving everything twice."

He stopped as though he realized he'd almost opened the door on the argument again.

"Well." He shrugged. "I suppose we can store it for a while."

"Trust me, Mr. Gladstone. This is my job. It's what I do, and I'm good at it. I can get top dollar for this place, but only if you let me do things my way."

Gladstone's expression was glum, but he managed to control his disappointment and forced a tight smile. "Of course, Ms. Neverall. You are the expert, after all."

Sandra nodded and smiled at him, the kind of indulgent smile that one might give recalcitrant children when they admit the error of their ways.

It was an expression I had seen often.

"Thank you, Mr. Gladstone," she said sweetly. "Now, if you'll excuse me? I'm sure you want to get back to supervising the packing, anyway."

She turned away, then turned back. "By the way, do you have that forwarding address for Miss Tepper? I would love to send her some flowers to brighten up her 'temporary quarters.'"

Gladstone patted the pockets of his jacket, and peered in the breast pocket of his shirt. He held up his hands and shrugged his shoulders. "It's here somewhere. I'll call you with it when I get back to the office."

I ducked back and sped down the hall to the bathroom. I didn't want my mother to know I had heard her exchange with Gladstone. Besides, I wasn't sure what the disagreement really meant, and I wanted time to think about it before I talked to her.

She found me, of course, her heels tapping through the house. The sound was muffled by the low hum of conversation among the movers, but I heard her approaching and quickly ducked under the bathroom sink.

I didn't have anything to actually do under the sink, but it was the safest place to hide. I could always pretend I was working, and she wouldn't know any better.

"Georgiana?" Her voice carried down the hall. "Where are you, dear? I saw your car outside . . ."

The tapping stopped, and I could see her latest acquisition at the door to the bathroom. Not Jimmy Choos, thank heavens, but close. A three-figure price tag instead of four. Even Sandra had her limits.

"Hi, Mom," I called from under the sink. I rattled a wrench and faked a little grunt of effort. "What's up?"

I wasn't sure what else to say, so I opted for nothing. It seemed the safest thing to do.

"Just checking on the progress here," she answered. "I had expected the house to be empty before now." She sighed. "But at least it's getting done. Now maybe we can get this place ready to sell."

"Well, that's good." I hesitated, but there was something I needed to ask her. "By the way, when you stopped by the other night, what was it you wanted?"

There was an awkward pause, and I wondered if she was going to answer my question. I saw her heels shuffle slightly, as though she was nervous.

"I just . . ." She coughed lightly. "Must be the smoke," she said. "Never could tolerate smoke."

I made a noncommittal hum that she could take for agreement, or sympathy, or whatever she chose, and waited for her to continue.

"It wasn't anything, really. Gregory was working late, and I was sort of at loose ends. I thought you might want to grab a bite to eat.

"But you had a date!" She sounded far too pleased at the prospect, but I let her keep her illusions. They were mostly harmless, after all.

What was more stunning was the idea of my mother actually asking me to have dinner with her. I was shocked.

"I'm sorry I was busy," I said from my hiding place. "That might have been fun."

To my surprise, I found that I really meant it. I had always wanted a good relationship with my mother, but I had never measured up, and she had never understood me.

Perhaps I never really understood her, either.

"Maybe another time?" I suggested.

"That would be good." Her heels scuffed the doorsill, as though she wasn't sure whether to stay or go.

She decided to go. "I've got work piled up at the office," she said, turning back to the hall. "I'll call you about dinner. Maybe one night next week."

"Sure. Just not Tuesday, okay?"

"Right, your class." Her stilettos disappeared from view, and I heard them tap-tap-tap down the hall.

I was just scooting out from under the sink when Barry walked in. He glanced down at me, and a knowing grin spread across his face.

"Your mother was here, right?"

I felt the color rise in my face as I stood up. "That obvious, huh?"

"Only to me," he reassured me. "Because I know you don't have a thing to do under there." He laughed. "At least my daughter doesn't hide from me."

"She's twelve, Bear. Give it time."

He shook his head. "We'll see."

He hefted his toolbox. "Let's go, Neverall. They finally got the basement clear, so we can start working down there, if your ankle is up to the stairs."

In answer, I picked up my toolbox from where I had dragged it under the sink with me and followed him down the hall and into the kitchen, to the basement door.

"Mind if I ask you a question before we get started?"

Barry looked at me, his brow furrowed. "As long as I can take the Fifth," he said.

I grinned. "Nothing like that, I promise." I shifted my toolbox from one hand to the other, stalling. Now that I had the chance, I hesitated. But I trusted Barry's judgment.

"What do you think of Gregory Whitlock?"

"He's smart," Barry answered. "One of the best heads for business in this town. He knows his stuff, that's for sure."

"Paula doesn't like him much," I said.

Barry smiled, affection for his wife shining in his eyes. "Paula is a very loyal friend," he said, as though that explained everything.

"Huh?"

"She thinks he's taking advantage of Martha Tepper with this deal." He motioned to the house, a gesture that seemed to encompass all of Miss Tepper's property. "She thinks her friend Martha is being taken for a ride by a sharpie, and she is rather, um, indignant about it."

"But you don't agree?" I found it hard to believe Barry was defending Gregory, knowing what his wife thought.

"Martha Tepper isn't a fool," he said. He lowered his voice. "I'm probably not supposed to know, but I have heard that Miss Tepper's attorneys drove a hard bargain on the two properties. She gets a slice of the profits from both deals, in return for a smaller up-front payment."

"So, why don't you tell her that? Let her know that he isn't taking advantage, that he and Miss Tepper are partners in the project?"

"Have you tried to persuade Paula Ciccone of anything?" Barry asked. "My wife, much as I adore her, gives a whole new meaning to the word *stubborn*. She is absolutely convinced that Whitlock is a crook, and nothing will change her mind."

Barry sighed. "I have learned, over the years, to pick my battles, just like any man that's been married very long.

"Don't get me wrong," he added hastily. "Paula is the best thing that ever happened to me. But under that sweet librarian, she's still the Italian spitfire I married."

I nodded. It had been a while since I had been in a serious relationship. There was one years back in San Francisco, and it had been a lie. But I remembered the part about choosing your battles. Some things just weren't worth stressing over.

The trick was to learn where your own personal limits were. I had discovered there was something worse than standing up for yourself, even if it meant an argument— not standing up for yourself.

"Thanks, Barry. Appreciate you telling me."

"No sweat," he said. "Just don't tell Paula, okay?"

I ran a finger across my lips in a zipping motion.

Ahead of us, the basement door stood open, a trail of dusty footprints attesting to the traffic in and out of the basement. The stairs descended into a murky blackness despite the morning sun.

Barry reached for the light switch at the top of the stairs and clicked it several times without success. "Bulb must be burned out," he said, taking a flashlight from his tool belt. "There's another light downstairs, but it isn't on this circuit. Wait 'til I get it on."

He started down the stairs, the bulky toolbox bumping against his leg as he took each step. The beam of the heavy flashlight bounced in the dark as he descended, and the stairs creaked under his weight.

Anyone else, I might have kidded about the noise, but on pizza night, Paula had told Sue and me how Barry was trying to lose weight. She said she hadn't had pizza in weeks, and had dug into the Garibaldi's box with gusto.

Besides, the moving crew had taken everything out of the basement earlier, dragging the oversized furniture, packed trunks, and heavy boxes up those wooden steps.

They had held a lot more than Barry already this morning. He was about halfway down when I heard another sound. Not a creak, but the distinct crack of splintering wood.

chapter 18

The beam from Barry's flashlight flew around the basement, its light alternately thrown on the concrete floor, the exposed ceiling beams, and the bare walls, before it crashed against the concrete and went out.

At the same time, I heard several other sounds: the clang and crash of Barry's toolbox, the clatter of tools spilling onto bare concrete, and the repeated muffled thuds of a large, soft object bouncing down the remaining steps.

"Barry!"

I reached for my own flashlight, playing the beam over the staircase and onto the floor.

At the bottom of the stairs I could see a Barry-shaped object in an unmoving heap.

My heart pounded and fear lanced through me, knotting my stomach into a fist.

I tried not to imagine the worst as I stood at the top of the stairs, but the still heap at the bottom turned my knees to jelly.

I forced back the growing panic and swallowed hard. Barry needed help, and that help was me.

I hurried down the stairs, silently cursing the fates that had seen fit to give us this job.

If we weren't being deliberately sabotaged, we must have the worst luck in the history of indoor plumbing.

I was voting for sabotage.

I stepped gingerly over the broken tread and raced down the remaining steps.

By the time I reached the bottom, the Barry-shaped lump was stirring.

He sat up, and looked blearily back up the staircase at the broken tread.

Then I heard something I had never heard on a job site before. Softly, almost whispered, I heard Barry Hickey curse. Not just a single expletive, but entire strings of them, conjugated and concatenated in truly amazing combinations.

The man had an extensive vocabulary—including all seven of George Carlin's forbidden words—and he was using them in ways I hadn't thought possible.

I listened in awe for what felt like several minutes, though it was probably only a few seconds.

Barry slowed down. He looked up at me, his expression unreadable in the dark basement. "You will not," he said, "tell Paula I said that."

"Said what?" I deadpanned.

To tell the truth, it was a virtuoso performance, one I couldn't have duplicated if I'd wanted to.

Which I didn't.

I whistled, long and low. "I gotta tell you, though. That was a very thorough appraisal of the situation."

"Thanks," he said. "Good to know those Navy years weren't wasted."

"Ah, so that's what swearing like a sailor sounds like. Good to know. But if you're through for the moment, let me ask. Are you okay?"

Barry moved carefully, patting himself and moving each limb. "Nothing broken," he said after several tentative stretches.

"I'm going to have some bruises, and I'll likely be stiff tomorrow." He glanced up. "Sort of like you are today."

I grimaced. Yes, I was stiff and sore. And now Barry would be, too.

"This job is jinxed," I said.

Barry waved off my offer of a hand and pulled himself to his feet.

With the help of my flashlight, we managed to find the cord for the single bare bulb in the basement, and turned on the light.

I helped Barry retrieve his tools, and we stowed them in the toolbox. Barry was favoring his right arm, and I put my hand on his shoulder to get him to stand still.

"Are you sure you're okay? That was a nasty fall. Maybe you ought to go see Dr. Cox." I consulted the battered plastic watch on my wrist. "He should be at Immediate Care about now."

Barry shook his head. "Don't need to," he said. "I've been bruised before. I don't need a doctor to tell me I didn't break anything."

"Ahem!" I cleared my throat loudly. "I beg your pardon, but didn't we just have this same conversation—what?— two days ago? And weren't you the one insisting that I had to go to the doctor because the injury occurred on the job?"

"That was different," Barry growled. He wriggled his shoulders and did a couple deep-knee bends to illustrate his point. "I can move just fine.

"Besides, I'm the boss, and I get to decide who has to go to the doctor, and who doesn't."

I thought he was making a mistake, but there was nothing more I could do. "All right," I muttered. "But I'm not going to be the one to explain to Paula why you didn't go to the doctor.

"Choose your battles, remember?"

"Point taken." He moved his toolbox over near the exposed drain pipes for the bathroom and began searching for a wrench in the jumble we had recovered from the floor. "I'll stop in and see Dr. Cox after lunch.

"Now can we get to work on this drain?"

By the time we had finished replacing the corroded pipe, it was nearly noon.

Upstairs the movers had stopped, the sudden silence a welcome relief after hours of scraping and thumping over our heads.

We emerged from the basement to find the house nearly empty. All that was left were bags of open food packages from the kitchen piled in a garbage can and an invoice copy left on the kitchen counter.

Everything else was gone.

So much for my plan to continue searching. If there was anything to discover in Martha Tepper's belongings, it was packed away in a storage facility somewhere under lock and key.

I glanced around once more, my heart sinking.

I turned to Barry, just in time to see him wince as he set his toolbox on the kitchen floor.

"You are going to Immediate Care, right?" I challenged.

"Yeah, yeah."

He left the toolbox by the sink and walked toward the open front door.

We had more work to do, but Barry moved as though each step was painful. I watched him shuffle toward the door, and realized he wouldn't be able to work anymore today.

"Barry." He stopped at the door, and looked back.

"Yeah?"

"What say we knock off for today? We aren't going to get finished here now, anyway. Let's just come back in the morning, after you've had some rest."

Barry hesitated.

"I could use the rest myself," I lied. The moving van was still at the curb but the crew had left for lunch before taking the truck to unload, and a plan was forming in my brain. "You go ahead. I'll clean up, and get things ready for tomorrow.

"I won't do anything I shouldn't," I added. "No work. Just cleaning and putting stuff away. I know the rules."

I waited, seconds ticking by. I didn't know how soon the moving crew would be back, and I needed Barry to get going.

Finally, he sighed. "You're probably right," he said.

I didn't give him the chance to change his mind.

"Good enough," I said. "You go see Dr. Cox, and take care of yourself." The hearty tone of my voice sounded fake to me. I hoped Barry wouldn't think so.

I headed back to the basement stairs. "I'll just get things ready for tomorrow, and I'll be out of here myself."

"Be sure it's locked up when you leave," he said.

"I will."

I waited on the stairs until I heard Barry's truck pull away, then ran through the house to the front door.

The moving van was still there, and the crew wasn't.

So far, so good.

An adjustable wrench hidden in my pocket bumped against my leg as I hurried toward the back of the moving van. It was part of my hastily concocted cover story, if I was caught in the back of the truck—my missing wrench had somehow gotten into one of the boxes of Martha Tepper's possessions.

The back of the truck was closed, but the padlock wasn't shut, and it was a simple matter to open the door and clamber inside.

I closed the door most of the way. In case someone came by, I didn't want to be spotted, but I wanted to be able to get it open again easily.

The truck was nearly full. Furniture lined the walls, and sealed boxes filled the spaces above, below, and in between the large pieces.

I wasn't sure where to start.

The boxes were out. I couldn't open them without arousing suspicion, and there wasn't time to go through each of them.

I settled for the dressers and nightstands, in the hopes

of finding some clue as to where Martha Tepper had gone.

And who had taken her there.

The dresser was shoved against the side of the truck, its drawers locked in place by a stack of boxes in front of it.

I pushed the boxes aside as far as I could. They moved slightly, giving me room to pull the drawers out a few inches.

It would have to do.

The bottom drawer held nightclothes—flannel gowns and cotton pajamas, and a worn chenille robe—along with a quilted electric heating pad.

I shoved the drawer closed and opened the next one. Jeans, T-shirts, a sweatshirt. Nothing useful.

Two drawers to go.

The next one had sweaters and several small white boxes.

I opened the first box and found a hinged jewelry box, with a pair of gold earrings inside.

The rest of the boxes also contained jewelry. To my untrained eye, it looked like good quality, though not extremely valuable.

But no woman would leave even her everyday jewelry behind. She would pack her earrings, necklaces, and bracelets, the things she'd wear regularly.

I grimaced, and kept searching.

The last drawer was underwear. Cotton panties, sturdy nylon bras. Nothing Victoria's Secret for Martha Tepper, thank heaven. If she had racy underwear, I really didn't want to know. The drawer was strictly Playtex and Hanes, to my immense relief.

There were no notes, no diaries, nothing to give me a hint of Miss Tepper's whereabouts.

But there was a clue, one I didn't want to have.

The drawers were full, every one of them. There were no clothes missing from Martha Tepper's dresser.

Martha Tepper had left town without so much as a change of underwear. She had left her jewelry, including the brooch that lay in Sue's desk drawer. She left food in the cupboard and sheets on the beds. She had left good-byes unsaid, and disappeared.

Rick and Rachel Gladstone wanted Martha's things left in the house. Wouldn't they need to send at least *some* of them to her? Didn't she need clothes and underwear and her everyday jewelry in her new life?

Another thought struck me, chilling me to the bone.

Whoever had made Martha disappear might be the same person responsible for all that had gone wrong on this job.

My hands shook as I closed the drawer and moved the boxes back in front of the dresser.

Back home, I couldn't relax.

I rummaged through the closet and found my gi. I hadn't worn it in several months, but today I needed the comfort of the traditional gear.

I slipped into the pants and wrapped the jacket around my chest, tightening the belt.

The suit settled on my body, calming me the way a child's favorite blanket offers security and comfort.

I don't know how long I practiced. The second bedroom of my rental had a heavily quilted mat on the floor, and I spent the rest of the afternoon tumbling and twisting until my mind emptied, and I regained some control.

My muscles screamed for rest, and I dropped to the mat. My ankle throbbed, reminding me of the punishment it had taken only a couple days earlier.

I dragged myself to the shower and then fell into bed. I was too exhausted to think, too worn out to care about anything.

As the song says, whatever gets you through the night.

Working with Barry the next morning was a strain. We were both stiff and sore, and neither one of us was moving very fast.

Worse, we were working in the basement renovating the waste lines, never a pleasant task.

And we were working on a job where accidents had become a daily occurrence, in spite of all the safety precautions we took—which were extensive. One of Barry's rules.

As renovation jobs go, this was better than most. We were in a basement, not a crawl space full of bugs and dirt and who-knows-what-else. We had electric lights rather than flashlights and battery work lamps, and we were dry, not crawling in mud and rain puddles.

But we were still working on pipes that ran overhead and we spent most of the morning reaching above our heads, disconnecting lines and fitting new pipes into the system.

My arms were rubbery with fatigue and I wondered if Barry was ever going to call a break. I needed coffee, and maybe something to eat.

I glanced at my watch. Ten more minutes. If Barry didn't call it, I would.

I watched him as he sweated the stretch of copper pipe I was holding in place. Although he would never admit it, he was hurting, too. Sweat beaded his face even though the basement was chilly, and the muscles in his arm quivered with the strain of holding them straight up.

When the join was complete, we strapped the pipe to the joist and tightened the screws. There was still one more connection, and it was in a tight corner where there wasn't much room to work.

"We've got to move that piece of drywall," Barry said, eyeing the corner. "I don't know why they hung drywall before we were through down here, but it's got to go if we're going to get that last run in place."

I groaned. Like digging trenches and lugging pipe, taking down the sloppily nailed piece of drywall was the job of the apprentice.

"Tell you what," Barry said, sweetening the pot. "You get that down, it's lunchtime—and I'm buying."

"I never turn down a free meal," I answered. "But are we talking real food or a visit to Mayor McCheese?"

Barry gave me a shocked look. "That *is* real food, girl! Don't you knock it. You show me what you got, and if I'm really impressed, we'll do Dee's Lunch."

"Deal."

I picked up the pry bar from my toolbox and wedged the end into the seam of the drywall. It was a tight squeeze. I looked around for something to pound it in, and spotted a stout two-by-four. Just what I needed.

I aimed the board at the end of the pry bar, and let fly. The bar moved a fraction of an inch, pulling up the drywall and spreading the seam open.

Focus. Remember your training. Concentrate all your energy into the blow.

There is a rule, somewhere, that tired people shouldn't be allowed to operate tools. Even simple ones like a pry bar and a hunk of two-by-four.

My concentration was fine. It was my aim that went awry. Instead of hitting the pry bar, my swing bounced off the edge of it. The pry bar fell to the floor, and I instinctively jumped away from the falling metal.

Years of training had taught me how to land, but my ankle was still tender and my steel-toed boots were not designed for graceful moves. Instead of taking a step back, I twisted around and lost my balance.

The end of the board rammed the drywall, punching a ragged hole in the wall. I slammed into the wall following the force of the blow, and my weight pushed against the two-by-four, dragging it down. The hole grew larger, a ragged tear down the sheet.

I jerked to a stop when the board hit a cross member of the stud wall that supported the drywall.

My breath came in short gasps, the aftermath of my sudden fall. I was still gripping the piece of two-by-four, my hand trembling with the backlash of an adrenaline surge. I couldn't make my fingers move to release the board.

Barry was next to me, although I had no memory of him moving. He put an arm around my waist and I leaned into him.

"Maybe we shouldn't have tried to work today," he said. "Using the pry bar and a hunk of wood"—he gently unwound my fingers from around the two-by-four— "was a pretty crazy choice. And I was too beat to stop you."

"I told you, Bear," I whispered, my voice too shaky to produce any volume, "this job is jinxed."

"I don't believe in jinxes and neither do you." He looked around the basement, as though he might find an explanation of the last few days. "But something is weird about this job, and I wish I knew what it was."

"I'm telling you," I said. "It's a jinx. Either that, or someone doesn't want us here.

"Do you think Miss Tepper has a ghost?"

Barry smiled thinly but the expression didn't reach his eyes, which remained dark and brooding.

He bent down to examine the damage to the wall. "We'll have to take care of this," he said.

I crouched down next to him, steadying myself with one hand on the wall. I peered into the hole, leaning close to see in the dark.

Maybe I was looking for answers, too.

What I wasn't looking for was the wad of black plastic stuffed inside the stud wall.

I'd read plenty of stories of people finding lost valuables and ancient treasures hidden in attics and basements.

How cool would it be to find something valuable? With the way our luck had been running, it was more likely to be old newspaper clippings, or unpaid bills, or a misplaced trash bag.

For a moment I let my imagination run free. It could be anything! Technically it would belong to Gregory Whitlock, or the Gladstones via Martha Tepper's power of attorney, however the papers read on the house. But it would still be exciting to be the person who found it, whatever it was.

"Barry, look at this!"

I reached carefully through the hole and grasped the edge of the plastic. I started pulling gently, working the plastic through the ragged hole in the drywall.

"Talk about sloppy." I tugged, and the plastic began to emerge from the hole. It was black, and heavyweight, like an industrial trash bag. "Looks like the contractors missed a bag of trash."

Barry shook his head in disgust. Some of the local building contractors were as meticulous as he was, but some were, well, not. It looked like the guys who did this job were in the "not" column.

"I wonder if they were trying to get rid of some asbestos?"

Asbestos abatement was a major issue in older buildings. The rules for removal and disposal were detailed, and the process was expensive and time-consuming. Contractors had been known to find creative means of disposing of the material, in order to avoid regulations and inspections they found intrusive.

Barry took the bag into the middle of the basement, directly under the overhead light fixture, and worked the knot in the top of the bag loose.

I leaned against the wall, waiting for him to inspect our discovery and trying to catch my breath. I was curious about the bag, but I was feeling a little unsteady, so I watched from a distance as Barry opened the top of the bag and peered in.

He stood immobilized for several seconds, staring at the contents.

"Georgie, you have your cell phone?"

I patted my overalls, then pulled the phone from an inside pocket. "Right here."

"Call the sheriff."

"Why? Sheriff Mitchell doesn't have anything to do with asbestos. That's the DEQ, isn't it?"

"It's not asbestos, Georgie. Call the sheriff. Now."

chapter 19

Sometimes, you have to act first and ask questions later.

I called the sheriff.

While I listened to the ringing at the other end of the line, I walked over to Barry.

He was still staring into the bag, and I tugged the top open enough to get a peek inside.

What I saw hollowed my stomach, and my knees went a little wobbly again. I looked up at Barry, and the shock on my face probably mirrored the look on his.

I reached into the bag, and Barry instantly batted my hand away. "Don't touch anything!" he hissed.

I yanked my hand back.

In the bottom of the bag was what looked like a very dirty towel. It had once been white, or perhaps pale pink. Now it was covered with large brownish-red splotches.

Spilled paint, I told myself. Or rust. But there was no brown or red paint anywhere in the house, and the churning in my stomach told me what my brain refused to admit.

Blood. Lots of it.

"Sheriff Mitchell here."

I had forgotten the phone clutched in my hand. When Sheriff Mitchell spoke, I jumped, my heart racing, and nearly dropped my phone.

The reception in the basement wasn't good, but I was too distracted to move.

Instead, I shouted into the phone. "We need you here, Sheriff. We found something!"

Sheriff Mitchell was clearly more accustomed to frantic phone calls than I was to finding bloody towels.

"Okay," he said, his voice low and calm. "I'll need to ask a couple questions, all right?"

I nodded, then realized he couldn't see me over the phone. "Uh-huh," I said.

"First of all, where is here? And second, who is we?"

"The Tepper place. The house, not the warehouse. And this is Georgiana Neverall."

"Georgiana? Wade Montgomery's girlfriend?"

"Yes, sir." I didn't bother to correct him about the girlfriend part.

"Wade told me you were concerned about Martha. He said I might hear from you.

"So, you say you found something?"

There was a trace of something in his voice, skepticism maybe? What had Wade told him?

"It looks like a bloody towel."

"Uh-huh." He didn't sound very concerned. "And you said 'we' found it, is that right?"

"Yes," I snapped.

Why wasn't this man taking me seriously?

"Who's there with you, Miss Neverall?"

"My boss, Barry Hickey. We're working on the plumbing. Talk to him, if you don't believe me."

I thrust the phone at Barry. "Here, you talk to him."

I was breathing hard, as though I had run several miles. Panic, fear, and anger battled for control of my emotions.

Barry took the phone but he kept a tight grip on the bag.

"Sheriff." Barry spoke quickly. "There's a situation here, and I think it needs your attention, pronto.

"We found a bag hidden inside a wall. There appears to be a bloody towel or rag stuffed in the bottom of it."

He listened for a minute. "No, it isn't paint and it definitely isn't accidental. It was stuffed between the studs in the basement, behind a piece of fresh drywall."

He waited another few seconds.

"Fine," he said. "We'll wait for you. And be careful coming down the stairs, there's a broken step about halfway down. Wouldn't want you getting hurt."

Barry handed my phone back. "He's on his way. Apparently your boyfriend said something to him, so he was expecting you to call." He chuckled grimly. "He wasn't expecting me to back you up, I don't think."

"He's not my boyfriend." This time I did correct the designation.

"Well, not after that," Barry said.

"Not at all," I said hotly.

Barry shrugged. "Well, clearly he told the sheriff something. But the man's on his way. He said not to touch anything while we're waiting."

Within a few minutes I could hear sirens approaching. They cut off suddenly, and several car doors slammed.

A voice called outside the front door. "Sheriff's department."

After a few seconds the door opened, and the tromp of booted feet echoed through the empty house overhead.

"Anybody here?" a male voice called out.

"Down here," Barry answered. "In the basement."

Dark boots appeared at the top of the stairs and started down. The boots belonged to a tall man with a graying buzz cut and ramrod-straight posture, dressed in a sharply creased khaki uniform with a wide Sam Brown belt creaking at his waist.

Fred Mitchell was an ex-Marine, and it showed.

"Watch out for the broken step," Barry reminded him.

The sheriff stepped carefully over the splintered tread

and turned to call back up to the men following him. "Broken step there. Baker, check it out, would you?"

After that, everything got a little crazy.

The sheriff immediately took possession of the plastic bag, though Barry seemed reluctant to relinquish control.

A clean plastic tarp was spread on the basement floor and a deputy carefully upended the bag onto the tarp. The towel tumbled out and several pieces of metal spilled from inside the towel, tinkling against the concrete floor under the thin plastic.

I'd watched enough crime shows on TV to know that they were shell casings, little tubes of tarnished brass.

Sheriff Mitchell pulled on a pair of latex gloves and took a pen from his pocket. Using the point of the pen, he picked up the edge of the towel. As he did, I could see that there were several large, irregularly shaped spots, smeared and streaked across the surface of the towel.

It looked like someone had used it to clean up blood.

The sheriff looked up at Barry. "Show me where you found this."

Barry showed him the hole in the wall and said a tool slipped. To my relief, he didn't explain exactly how the tool slipped or that I was the sole culprit.

While they were talking, I heard a familiar voice at the top of the stairs, arguing with one of the deputies that he had to be allowed in the basement. Sheriff Mitchell had called him.

Wade poked his head through the door at the top of the stairs. "Fred? Would you tell your deputy it's okay to let me come down?"

The sheriff waved at the deputy. "Let him by."

Wade hurried down the stairs, stepping gingerly over the splintered tread where Deputy Baker—according to Fred Mitchell—was inspecting the broken wood.

When Wade reached the bottom of the stairs, he rushed over and threw an arm around my shoulders. "Are you okay?"

Mitchell glanced over. "Hi, Montgomery." His gaze

moved over to me for a second. "Thought your boyfriend might want to know what happened," he said before going back to his conversation with Barry.

"He's not my boyfriend," I protested.

Mitchell looked back and raised an eyebrow at Wade, but didn't say anything.

"We can talk about that later," Wade whispered. "What I want to know is how you are?"

"How do you *think* I am?" I shouted. "I'm right here, safe and sound—except that nobody wants to take me seriously. It's not me you should be worried about." I looked around at the group of men crowding the basement. "I'm not the one that's been missing for weeks. And I'm not the one with bloody towels and shell casings hidden in my basement. Martha Tepper's the one you should be worrying about."

"And I am," Sheriff Mitchell said. His voice was quiet, but the air of authority was clear. This was the guy in charge, and everyone turned to listen to him.

"As of now, I want this place secured while we test these." He waved at the towel and the shell casings.

He turned to Barry. "No more work, at least for a couple days, okay?"

I groaned. "My mother is going to pitch a fit!"

"Your mother?" The sheriff looked at me. "What does your mother have to do with anything?"

"My mother is Sandra Neverall, of Whitlock Estates Realty. She and her"—I hesitated—"partner are the ones who commissioned the renovations on the house. They've been pushing to get the work done so they can resell it."

Barry looked from the wall to me, and back again. "I'll call Whitlock," he volunteered. "Tell him there's a delay, and we're going to switch over to the warehouse for a couple days."

"Let's get you out of here," Wade said, pulling me toward the stairs.

Sheriff Mitchell looked over at Wade. "I'll want to talk to her," he told him, as though I wasn't standing right there. "Can you bring her by my office later this afternoon?" He consulted the bulky watch on his wrist. "About three?"

Wade shot me a warning look as I started to open my mouth. "We'll be there," he answered before hurrying me up the stairs and out of the house.

We reached the front door before I had a chance to say anything more.

"What was that all about?" I demanded. "Couldn't I speak for myself?"

Wade took me by the elbow and guided me toward the Beetle. He opened my door and practically shoved me into the car. "Meet me at Franklin's and I'll buy you lunch."

Wade walked away before I could agree. His assumption that I'd meet him where he said to was annoying, but there was still that "boyfriend" thing. I needed to set him straight, and fast.

I arrived at Franklin's ahead of Wade and snagged a table by the window, where I could watch for him. It gave me a tiny edge in the confrontation I was sure was coming.

When Wade slid into the booth across from me, I was ready for him. "What's with this 'girlfriend/boyfriend' thing, Wade? I thought we had agreed to take it slow and see what happens."

Wade colored and wiggled nervously in his seat. "It was the simplest way to describe you," he said. "I didn't want to go into the whole old-friends-who-are-dating-casually thing with Mitchell." He shrugged. "Besides, I think we're being exclusive, aren't we? So, it's not too far from the truth."

He waved the subject away. "Anyway, we have more important things to discuss right this minute."

The waitress chose that moment to interrupt us for our lunch order. I made a random sandwich choice, and coffee. Wade ordered a burger. Neither one of us seemed to care much about what we ate.

"So what's more important, Wade? What was it we couldn't talk about in front of anyone?"

Wade still looked uncomfortable, but his lips drew into a determined line and he held my gaze. "What were you doing out there, Georgie?" he asked angrily.

"What was I doing?!?" I shouted. Heads turned from the counter, and I bit my lip. I balled my hands into fists below the edge of the table and forced myself to lower my voice to a conversational level.

"What was I doing? I was doing my job, Wade. I was out there *with my boss*, working on the plumbing. I was there because that was where the work was. Why are you having difficulty with that concept?" I was having difficulty stopping myself from reaching for his throat.

Wade glanced around as though afraid someone might be watching. The people at the counter had gone back to their lunches, and the waitress was busy at the other end of the room. No one was paying any more attention to us.

"No one's looking, Wade," I said. "They all know it's just Doc Neverall's nutty daughter. You know, the one that went away to that fancy school and then decided to come back here and be a plumber."

Bitterness rose in my throat and I washed it back down with a gulp of scalding coffee.

"I've heard them. This is a small town, as you remind me. Often. Everybody has an opinion, and a lot of them are quite happy to share it with you whether you want to know or not."

Wade sighed and stared into his coffee cup. He stirred it idly, even though he had added neither cream nor sugar.

"I'm sorry," he said at last. "You're right, and I didn't mean to be one of 'those people.'"

Our sandwiches arrived, and Wade sat mute until the waitress left again. He shoved his plate to one side, ignoring the food.

"I'll be blunt, Georgie. Just listen, okay? Sheriff is an elected position. Like it or not, Fred Mitchell has to get

himself reelected every four years if he wants to keep doing the job."

"This is about politics?" I couldn't decide if I was confused, or just disgusted.

"It has to be. Mitchell's a good sheriff. He's honest, he
runs a clean department, and he gets the job done. But
there is always the cloud of another election hanging over
everything he does." Wade shrugged, and pulled his plate
back in front of him. "It's just a fact of life for him."

"So, he didn't want to think anything bad about Miss
Tepper's leaving because . . ." I let my sentence trail off.

Wade picked up the thought. "Because any kind of major crime is bad for his campaign. Don't misunderstand,"
he went on. "If there's evidence of anything, he'll be all
over it. The only thing worse than a serious crime, from
his point of view, is an unsolved crime.

"When I told him you were my girlfriend, Georgie, I
was telling him he should take you seriously. If you came
to him with something, I was vouching for you."

He smiled.

"Besides, I was kind of hoping maybe we were moving
in that direction. At least a little."

Wade took a bite out of his burger and waited for my
reaction.

I filed his comment away to examine later.

Right now, though, I had to concentrate on the more
pressing problem: the thing we had found hidden in Martha Tepper's basement.

"Okay. I'll cut the sheriff some slack. He's not a bad
guy. Blah, blah, blah. And apparently you were just trying
to help." I nodded quickly. "I get it. So what should I do?"

Wade swallowed and I picked up my sandwich. It was
my turn to wait, and I took a bite. Egg salad. Somehow,
I'd ordered an egg salad sandwich.

I hate egg salad.

"You have to go talk to the sheriff"—he glanced at his
watch—"in about an hour. Tell him everything you know,

and then stand back and let him do what he was elected to do. I promise you he's good, and he'll get to the bottom of this."

He picked up his burger and gave me a hard look. "Do you think you can do that?"

I thought about what he'd asked as I forced myself to chew and swallow the gooey, disgusting sandwich.

"I can," I said softly. "Within reason. I'm not going to tell him anything that's going to get me in trouble."

Wade struggled to keep a straight face, and I knew he was thinking about the night he had caught Sue and me outside Martha Tepper's house.

"Yeah," I said. "Self-incrimination is so not my style."

"Good idea," Wade said. He took another bite of burger, apparently having exhausted his supply of advice.

I shrugged and went back to my lunch. The fries were good, and I found myself taking another bite of the sandwich. It was still egg salad, but for food I hated, it wasn't too repulsive.

We ate quickly and I managed to finish half the sandwich. I kept looking at my watch as I wolfed down the fries and drained the refill of my coffee cup.

"Dogs?" Wade asked, when I glanced at my wrist for the fourth or fifth time.

"Yeah. I really need to let them out before I go talk to Sheriff Mitchell. No telling when I'll get back."

Wade nodded and signaled the waitress over. "Just put this on my tab, would you, Mary?"

"Sure."

After she left, Wade tossed a few singles on the table for a tip and stood up. "I'll meet you at your place," he said. "You let the dogs out and then I'll drive you over to the sheriff's office."

I stood, and led the way out the door. Once we were alone, I turned to face Wade.

"I can get there by myself," I said. "I'm sure you have things you need to do."

Wade studied me for a minute, and I thought I might have hurt his pride. Still, I felt like this was something I should take care of myself.

Besides, if he took me to the sheriff's office, it would cement that boyfriend/girlfriend thing in everyone's mind, and I was pretty sure I didn't want that label. Not yet.

"You sure?"

I shook my head. "I promise I'll go like a good little girl, Wade. Believe me, I can follow orders when I have to."

Wade agreed, reluctantly, to let me go alone. He made me promise to call him afterward. I just didn't say how soon afterward.

Which was probably a good idea.

The dogs were happy to see me, but Daisy quickly realized that they were getting only a few minutes in the backyard, and she gave me a look that clearly said I was committing Airedale neglect.

She was right, too. Since I'd become involved with the mystery of Martha Tepper's disappearance, I hadn't been giving them the attention they deserved.

"I swear," I told them as I brought the dogs in and gave them green treats, "as soon as my visit to the sheriff is done, I am through with this. Then I'll take you on long walks and we'll go see Sue for a shampoo."

I tickled Buddha behind his ears and hugged Daisy. "It's all over. I promise."

The sheriff's office was in a low, brick-and-glass, 1960s-modern building two blocks from Main Street. As a kid I'd been confused when someone referred to it as the "new" sheriff's office—it had always been there. But as an adult I realized it was decades newer than Main Street.

Sheriff Mitchell was on the phone when I arrived, and the deputy at the counter showed me to a small, sparsely furnished office to wait for him.

I sat in the chair he indicated, an ancient metal frame with a cracked, dark green, vinyl seat and back. The padding had packed down somewhere in the Reagan Administration, and though it still seemed sturdy, it offered little in the way of comfort.

Then again, I don't think comfort was a high priority.

The only other furniture in the room was a bare wooden desk of about the same vintage as my chair and a spindly looking secretary's chair in one corner.

I was wondering if the sheriff intended to sit on the secretary's chair—there wasn't much else to do in the bare room—when the door opened. Fred Mitchell wheeled in a high-backed executive chair, the kind I'd used to have in my San Francisco office. I remembered that when you have a really good chair, you take the time to drag it with you to meetings.

I supposed this qualified as a meeting of some sort. What it really was, of course, was an interrogation. I just didn't want to think about that part of it.

The sheriff moved a file folder off the seat of the chair, sat down, and placed the file in the exact center of the desk. He took a small tape recorder out of his shirt pocket and laid it on the desk, next to the file.

"Do you mind?" he said, pointing at the recorder. "I'm pretty good at notes, but this makes sure I have an absolutely accurate record of what was said."

Alarm bells went off in the back of my head. "Is this an official interview? Should I have a lawyer?"

Sheriff Mitchell leaned over the desk. His dark eyes were wide and his voice soft and sincere as he replied. "This is unofficial, and the recording is just for my use in the investigation. You don't need a lawyer, and I'll tell you if we reach a point where you might.

"For now I just need to find out what you know—anything that might help us discover what really happened to Martha Tepper."

There it was. *What really happened.* That didn't sound like he believed she'd moved to Arizona after all.

"You mean . . . ?"

The sheriff avoided my question. "The bag you found

in the Tepper house contained some objects that have aroused our interest. We are doing a preliminary inquiry.

"Mr. Hickey gave us his version of what happened, and I'd like to hear yours."

I tried to remember all the advice I had ever heard about talking to the police. Answer politely, tell the truth, don't volunteer information.

I chose my words carefully, giving him the bare facts of our discovery that morning. I didn't go into detail about how a tool had gone through the wall—it was just an accident.

The sheriff asked if I had seen or heard anything unusual during the last couple weeks while I was working at the house.

I stopped to think, and the miniature recorder stilled. The sheriff saw me look at it, and the corners of his mouth lifted slightly. "Voice activated. Saves on batteries."

I didn't tell him I knew a lot about the technology. Samurai Security had used voice activation recording when necessary, and we'd perfected a couple nifty tricks. Tricks that Blake and his buddies were now using, I was sure.

The sheriff cleared his throat, drawing my thoughts back to the present. "Miss Neverall? Anything unusual?"

I decided the arguments between Sandra, Gregory, and the Gladstones didn't qualify as unusual. In fact, they had sounded pretty much business as usual, if you ask me.

But Janis Breckweth, that was definitely unusual.

"There was this woman," I said. How could I describe Janis Breckweth without making her sound like a nut case? Then again, maybe she really was a nut case.

I figured it was the sheriff's job to figure that out.

"She came to the house one day while Barry—Mr. Hickey—and I were working. She said she lived there, and she'd come to get her things."

"What can you tell me about her?"

"She looked kind of, I don't know, disheveled, I guess.

Her hair was a mess and it looked like she'd slept in her clothes. She said her name was Janis, and she was Martha Tepper's housekeeper."

The sheriff wrote down each detail as I told him, occasionally going back to underline or circle some particular piece of information.

Watching him take notes was nerve-wracking. My stomach clenched and I fought back the taste of egg salad rising in my throat.

I really hate egg salad.

"This Janis, you say her last name was Breckweth, right? She lived in that house?"

I nodded. "She said she'd lived there six years. A friend of mine, who knows Miss Tepper better than I do, told me Miss Breckweth had been living there for several years, so I guess it's true."

"And she said she came to get her belongings? She didn't take them with her when she left?"

I shrugged. "All I know is what Janis told me. She said a woman came and told her they were selling the house, and she had to leave. Said they wouldn't even let her wait until morning, or pack her clothes, or anything.

"That's all I know about her."

The recorder clicked off and the sheriff waited, as though he expected me to remember something else.

I could hear the clicking of computer keys from the other room, and the occasional muffled squawk of the police radio. Neither sound was loud enough to activate the recorder.

We sat for what felt like several hours in silence. The sheriff reviewed his notes, stopping to scribble things in the margins of the page as though he had all the time in the world.

Or as if he was waiting for something.

As the silence stretched, I found my palms sweating, and my heart beating faster. I had nothing to hide—well, almost nothing, and I'd had a key, so it really wasn't a break-in—but I was still reacting to the tension. I tried to imagine how nervous I would be if I had something serious I didn't want to share with him.

It reinforced what I had realized several days earlier: I was not cut out for a life of crime. Even vicarious crime. I wanted to confess to something, anything, just to break the silence.

Of course, I didn't have much to confess to, but that didn't stop me from wanting to. I wondered how real criminals handled this kind of treatment. On the other hand, real criminals probably didn't care.

The thought didn't help.

I considered telling him about the sabotage at the Tepper house. Was that significant? Would he care, or would I just sound paranoid? Probably the latter.

I kept quiet. No sense destroying what little credibility I had.

I did think of something, though. The sheriff probably wouldn't take it any more seriously than Barry or Wade had, but at least there was something I could say.

"It's probably nothing," I said, even though I didn't believe it. "But there was something else. I only just remembered it because it was at the warehouse, not Miss Tepper's house. She left all her furniture in the house, along with a lot of clothes and things, but this was at the warehouse."

The sheriff looked up from his notes. "You never know what might be important. Please, I want to hear anything you know."

"Well, there was this brooch." The recorder whirred, and I told him about finding the brooch in the trap of the utility sink at the warehouse.

"She wore that brooch every single day," I said. "That was why I was worried about her in the first place. She never went anywhere without it."

I hesitated. There was that whole thing about not volunteering information, but maybe that was just with lawyers, not police. Besides, I'd been worried about Martha Tepper for too long to stop now.

I told him the story of the brooch, the one Paula had told Sue and me, complete with the missing brother, the dead fiancé, and the dream to visit the Wall.

By the time I'd finished, I have to admit, I was a little choked up. I don't care what Wade said, it was a sad story.

"So," Sheriff Mitchell said when I ran down, "you don't think she would have left without that piece of jewelry?"

I shook my head. "Not a chance. I don't know her as well as some of the people around here, but I can't imagine any woman leaving a piece like that behind, any more than a married woman would leave her wedding ring."

"You'd be surprised," he said, in a tone that implied a lot, but he didn't say anything more.

I tried to remember if I had heard anything about the sheriff's current marital state, but my brain refused to cooperate. It was busy with more important things, like controlling the impulse to scream, "Let me out of here!"

"You don't agree." It was a statement, not a question. There was no point in asking when his answer was clear.

It was apparently my day to be wrong about everything.

"On the contrary, Georgiana—May I call you Georgiana?—I agree with you entirely. A piece that carries that much emotional and sentimental value does not get left behind except in a life-threatening emergency. And sometimes not even then.

"I have seen people run back into burning buildings or crawl into a smashed-up car, to retrieve a baby's toy or a favorite sweater. It's a stupid thing to do, but it happens."

He leaned back in his chair. "So I agree with you, Georgiana."

He lapsed back into silence and I tried not to fidget. We went on for several more minutes like that: long silences, with the recorder springing to life when Mitchell asked an occasional question.

At last the sheriff leaned forward. He steepled his fingers on the desk and stared down at his notes. "Is there anything else you can think of? Anything we ought to know?"

I shook my head. "I really think I told you everything I could remember."

"All right." He stood up.

A deputy, a different one than had been at the desk, came into the room at once, as though he had been waiting for some signal from the sheriff. He handed his boss a few sheets of paper and stepped back, waiting by the door.

I felt silly being the only one sitting down, so I stood up, too. I made no move to leave since no one had actually said I could go yet, and leaving without permission struck me as a bad idea.

The sheriff read the papers, flipping one over to read the back. I watched, not sure what to expect. Did he have some information about what we'd found?

"A couple things before you go, Georgiana. I'd like you to bring that brooch in here, please. It's lost property at the very least, and it may be evidence if we decide a crime has been committed."

"Sure," I said. "Right away."

The sheriff nodded once. "There are a couple reporters out front, claiming they want to get 'your side' of the story. You are welcome to speak to them, of course. But if you'd like to avoid them, Deputy Carruthers can show you the employee exit around back."

I'd dealt with the hyenas of the business press during the trouble at Samurai Security. A couple local reporters shouldn't be a problem. But I'd elect to avoid them if I could.

"Thanks. I'd appreciate that."

He handed over a picture and asked me if I knew the woman in the photo. It was Janis Breckweth. I identified her as the woman who came to the house and claimed to live there.

"I'll have her picked up," he said. "According to this report"—he tapped the piece of paper in his hand—"she's the new cook at Second Chances."

"That's a weird coincidence," I said. "I think that's where the crew came from that packed up Miss Tepper's house and took everything to storage."

Sheriff Mitchell shot me a hard look. "Are you sure?"

I nodded. I'd seen the Second Chances logo on the shirts the movers wore, and I remembered the Gladstones talking about them.

Mitchell glared and scrawled a note on the edge of the paper. "I don't believe in coincidence," he growled.

"Sorry."

"Not your fault." He waved away my apology and skimmed over one more piece of paper before sticking the entire stack into the file folder with his notes from our interview.

"Carruthers will show you the back exit, Georgiana. I'll see you back here later today?" His voice rose in a polite question, but I knew it was more than a request. "With that brooch."

He hesitated. "We did get some preliminary results from the lab," he said. "I suppose you deserve to know.

"Those were blood stains on the towel. DNA testing will take a while, but the type matches Martha Tepper's."

6

◆

never skimp on preparation

When it comes to tools, buy the best you can afford, not what looks nice. Good tools are worth every penny. Poor-quality tools make any job more difficult and prone to disaster.

—A Plumber's Tip from Georgiana Neverall

chapter 20

I tried to absorb what the sheriff had said as Carruthers led me down a short hallway, past several closed doors, and around a corner.

Ahead of us, a security door with a heavy lock and a crash bar blocked the end of the corridor.

Carruthers pulled a business card from his shirt pocket and handed it to me. "If it's a slow news day, the city paper will send someone out from the metro desk. They'll be hanging around the front. If you'd rather avoid them when you come back, just give me a call and I'll let you in this door."

"Thank you, Deputy. I just may take you up on that."

He swiped a key card through the slot next to the door, and we waited as the device clicked a couple times and then a green light appeared on the panel.

He pushed on the crash bar and held the door open for me.

"Call when you're ready to come back in, miss."

The "miss" was a nice touch. I'd been getting the occasional "ma'am" over the last year or so, and had begun to worry that I needed to rethink my mother's advice about wrinkle cream. But maybe not.

I hurried out into the late afternoon sun, relieved to be away from the oppressive atmosphere of the sheriff's station. Even though I hadn't been there as a suspect, I had still felt the walls closing in on me the entire time I was inside.

I skirted the parking lot, keeping an eye on the front door. Having successfully ducked the reporters, I didn't want to run into them before I reached my car.

By the time I got home, my phone had rung several times. I ignored it, concentrating on my driving, trying not to think about what I had learned.

In spite of the sheriff's careful words and his caution about DNA testing, I knew that was Martha Tepper's blood on the towel. A lot of it.

He hadn't said anything about the shell casings. No matter what they showed on TV, though, I was pretty sure the examination of those would take more than the couple of hours he'd had since we'd found them. But just the fact that they were there was a bad sign.

In my bedroom I dug in my jewelry box and pulled out the brooch I'd retrieved from Sue's office last week. It hadn't changed in the days since I had put it there, yet it felt different somehow—heavier.

I was the one who had changed. I knew more about the brooch and about its owner's fate than I wanted to.

The spent casings, the blood, the bag hidden in the wall—they were all things I would never forget.

Added together, they forced a conclusion I tried to avoid. Martha Tepper had been badly hurt, and the person who had hidden the bag was the last person to see her.

Alive.

I checked my cell phone before I got back in the car. Two calls from Sue, one from Paula, and three from my mother. As I scanned the call list, the phone rang again.

Make that four calls from Mom.

I considered letting it go to voice mail again, but I

knew I would have to talk to her eventually. Might as well get it over with.

"Georgiana? What have you gotten yourself into now?"

"Why, I'm fine, Mother. Thank you for asking. I was a bit upset, but I think I'll be okay."

"Don't be that way, Georgiana." My mother never appreciated my sarcasm. "Your boss would have told me if there was anything wrong with you. He just said you had to suspend work on the Tepper house because the police were there."

"They were."

"Georgiana!" I held the phone away from my ear, but I could still hear her exasperated voice. "You still haven't answered my question!"

"There isn't much to say, Mom. We found something we thought the sheriff might want to see, so we called him. He said he needed to investigate and told us to stop work for a couple days."

"But that's going to throw our renovation schedule off. How long will we have to wait?"

"I really don't know, Mother. That's the sheriff's call, not mine. I don't have anything to do with any of this."

"But you were right there. Barry said you were the one who found—what exactly did you find?"

"I can't talk about it, Mother." The sheriff hadn't actually said that, but it made a good excuse not to discuss with her what we'd found.

"Even with me, Georgiana? I'm your mother."

"No, Mom. I really can't tell you anything right now. As soon as I can, I'm sure you'll be one of the first to know."

She harrumphed into the phone, but she stopped arguing. "Very well, if that's how you're going to be."

"It's how I have to be for now, Mother. I have to go."

"You'll call me when you know something, won't you, Georgiana? Please?" There was a note of concern in her voice, and I relented.

"Yes, Mom, I will. I promise."

I finally got her off the phone and hurried out to the car. As I turned the key in the ignition, I realized I didn't know where to park once I returned to the sheriff's office.

I took Deputy Carruthers's card from my purse and gave him a call. He answered on the first ring.

"Come around the back," he said. "There's a lot marked for employees. You can park there, close to the back door."

"Great," I said. "I'm leaving my house right now, so I'll be there in a few minutes. I'll call you as soon as I get to the parking lot."

I found the lot he'd described, and phoned Carruthers again. A couple minutes later, he met me at the door.

"The sheriff's talking to someone right now," he said apologetically. "But you can wait, or you can just give me what you brought, if you want."

I considered the options. I wanted to find out if the sheriff had heard anything else, but I didn't want to have to sit around the office, waiting for him.

"Do you know anything more?" I asked Carruthers.

"No." He shook his head. "The lab is working and we're conducting an investigation. Beyond that, there isn't any information we're releasing."

I realized I was getting the brush-off.

Well, wasn't that what I wanted, to be relieved of any responsibility?

Still, I was curious about what was going on. I was involved, whether I had wanted to be or not, and I couldn't just walk away.

"I suppose I could give you the brooch," I said. I reached into my pocket, drawing it out. I looked at it, weighed it in my hand. It was just a piece of jewelry.

I held it out to Carruthers. He took a plastic bag from his pocket and pulled the top open so I could put the brooch inside.

"I found it in a drain pipe," I told him. "I cleaned it up. I wouldn't have done it if I'd known . . ." My voice trailed off. I didn't quite know what else to say.

Carruthers sealed the bag and wrote on it. "I'll see that this gets to the sheriff," he said. "Don't worry about cleaning it up. You had no way of knowing."

I turned to go.

A door opened in the hall ahead and Janis Breckweth emerged, followed by Sheriff Mitchell. She glanced my way, then did a double take as she recognized me. "You were there," she said. "You helped me get my things from Martha's house."

The sheriff tried to guide her toward the front door. "I can have a deputy take you home, Miss Breckweth. If you'll just wait a minute—"

"I can take her." The words were out of my mouth before I thought about what I was saying.

The sheriff looked at me, his eyebrows raised in question.

"I was just leaving," I said quickly. "I can drop Miss Breckweth off on my way home."

"You sure? I can have a deputy . . ."

"Sure." I motioned toward the back door. "Deputy Carruthers has that item you asked for, Sheriff. If there isn't anything else right now, I'd be glad to give Miss Breckweth a ride. Second Chances, right?" I turned to Janis. "I hear you're the new cook over there."

She smiled, but it didn't reach her eyes. "Needed a job, didn't I, and they gave me one. Place to stay, too. Maybe not as nice as Martha's house, but it'll do."

She held her chin up as though daring anyone to think less of her for living in the homeless shelter. There was a toughness to her that I hadn't seen the first time we'd met.

She wasn't a nut case; of that much I was suddenly certain.

Janis didn't speak until we were in the car and well away from the sheriff's office.

"He thinks I hurt Martha," she said without preamble. Her voice trembled with indignation. "As though I would hurt her! I was more like a sister to her than an employee, was what she always said.

"And now that nasty sheriff thinks I had something to do with her going away."

I shifted gears and made a tight left turn onto Main Street. Although there was little traffic, Main was about the slowest way back to Second Chances, and I wanted the opportunity to talk to Janis. Next to Paula Ciccone, she probably knew Martha the best.

"Well, you had a right to be upset, didn't you? I mean, she was going to sell out and move to Arizona. You'd be out of a job if she left, and have no place to live once she was gone.

"That would sure make me angry."

"I admit, I didn't like it much when she first started talking about it. She even offered to take me with her, but I hate the desert. I wasn't going to that godforsaken place for anybody, even Martha."

"So you were angry?" I risked a quick glance over at my passenger to gauge her reaction.

"At first, like I said. But it didn't matter anymore, since she wasn't going to go."

Janis dropped that bombshell as though it was an established fact, even though no one else in town seemed to be aware of it.

I concentrated on not running off the road as I reassessed my whole not-a-nut-case opinion.

"But how can you say that?" I asked. I hoped my voice didn't betray me; I was white-knuckling the wheel, trying not to consider the possibility that I was currently driving around with a lunatic in my car.

"She told me," Janis said calmly. "How could she, after she found out what those people were doing with her money?"

The surrealism level climbed another notch, and I swallowed hard. "What people?" I asked, fearful of the answer.

"You were there," she said. "The ones that were in the house with you."

"There were a lot of people in the house that day." Silently, I repeated, "Not the real estate people, not the real estate people . . ."

"That woman, the one that threw me out of the house," Janis said. "Her and her husband. You know, the whiny ones."

I nearly choked with relief. I didn't think my mother was capable of hurting anyone, but I still had my doubts about Gregory.

Even so, it was nice to get confirmation. You could call my mother a lot of things, many of them uncomplimentary, but you could never call her whiny.

"You mean the Gladstones?" I asked.

"Yes," Janis said. "Those lawyers. Martha said they were doing things with her money and she couldn't leave until she got them straightened out."

I was nearing the Second Chances building, and I slowed to turn into the parking lot.

"She was going to fire them if they didn't straighten up."

"Are you sure that's what she said?" Janis Breckweth might be a suspect, but she could still be telling the truth. And if Martha Tepper had a problem with money, I knew who could confirm it for me.

If he would.

"That's what she said. And it's what she wrote down."

"Wrote down?" This time my voice did squeak. I couldn't help it.

I lurched the Beetle into a parking space and killed the engine. I pretended it was deliberate.

"Wouldn't say it if it wasn't so, would I?" Janis challenged, turning to face me.

"Of course not." To tell the truth, I had no freakin' idea whether she'd say it or not, but I wasn't about to argue with her.

"Right." She crossed her arms over her scrawny chest. "She started writing it all down, keeping track of stuff. She was going to take care of it before she left."

"Wh-where did she write it down?"

"In that diary of hers. She started doing that a few weeks back, and she was always scribbling in it."

"She had a diary?"

"Just said that, didn't I? Are you even listening to me, girl? You're like that sheriff, only hear what you want."

"I, uh, I'm sorry," I stammered. Clearly, my interrogation technique could use some fine-tuning. "I was surprised, is all.

"So she was writing down all this stuff in a diary?"

Janis eyed me suspiciously for a few long seconds, then accepted my explanation.

"Yep. She always said she could write a book about the people in this town, and that's what I thought she was doing. But no, she was writing stuff about her lawyers and how she thought they were cheating her."

"Uh, Janis, why didn't she go to the police if she thought they were stealing?"

"All the bad things she was saying about them, she didn't really know if it was them for sure. She said she had to give them a chance to explain, and to fix things."

I nodded. That sounded like Martha Tepper, always trying to see the good side of people.

"Makes sense. But where is the diary now?"

"Someplace safe," she hedged. "Bet those lawyers would like to know. But it's someplace nobody is going to get it."

"What about the sheriff?" I asked. "Don't you think he ought to know about it?"

"What for?" Her mouth twisted, and for a second I thought she was going to spit, right there in my car.

"He just wants to make me out to be some crazy old lady who got mad at Martha and hurt her."

"But you didn't," I coaxed.

"Course not. Why would I? Martha said she would take care of me before she moved for good, that she'd see I was set up somewhere else. Even said she'd help me get moved."

Janis leaned over and looked deep into my eyes.

"That's why I knew she was coming back," she said with conviction. "She didn't do any of those things, and she promised. Martha always kept her promises. Always. So I knew she'd be back."

Judging from what the sheriff had told me and what I'd seen in the Tepper basement, I didn't think Martha was coming back, no matter how hard Janis believed.

Martha wasn't Tinkerbelle, and wishing and hoping weren't going to bring her back. But I wasn't going to be the one to say so to Janis.

"Still"—I pushed back a little—"the sheriff ought to know she was having trouble with the lawyers. That might be important."

Janis shook her head. Even though I pleaded with her for several more minutes, she wouldn't budge. She had the diary; I was sure of that. But she wasn't giving it up, and she refused to even consider telling the sheriff.

"I have supper to cook," she said, climbing out of the car. "The men count on me." There was stubborn pride in her voice once again. Janis Breckweth was a survivor, but not at the expense of other people.

As revealing as our meeting had been, I still had two new burning questions. Where was Martha Tepper's diary?

And who had her money?

chapter 21

I knew where the diary was, of course. Janis had it. But she wasn't telling anyone where she'd hidden it.

If I believed the rest of what she told me—and I did—someone Martha Tepper trusted had cheated and betrayed her. Someone with access to her finances had stolen from her.

I told myself there were lots of people with access to her money. The Gladstones were the most likely suspects, of course. According to Janis, Martha knew that but she wasn't one hundred percent sure. There was also the manager of the bank, and maybe an investment counselor. I'd heard lots of horror stories about stockbrokers and the like, churning the investments of clients, raking in huge commissions while the clients' funds dwindled.

And there was, I had to admit, her accountant.

Wade.

How much did I know about Wade? Not the Wade from high school, the Wade that Sue claimed moped when I left for college, but the right-now Wade, the one who had bought a house near Martha Tepper. The one who knew I

had been snooping around the Tepper house. The Wade
I'd shared my suspicions with.

The Wade who pooh-poohed my concerns and dis-
missed my fears.

So, how much did I really know about him?

Enough.

My mother trusted him, and she didn't trust much of
anyone after Dad died. What's more, she trusted Wade
with her money. That alone made him above reproach.

As though to prove it to myself, I found myself parking
on the street directly in front of Wade's office.

Put your money where your mouth is, Neverall.

Wade was on the phone when I walked in. He smiled at
me and signaled to the chair across from his desk, holding
up a finger in the universal "just one minute" gesture.

It was one I knew well; I had used it a lot myself, back
when I was running Samurai. Back then, everyone waited
for me.

Wade looked genuinely pleased to see me.

"What brings my favorite plumber to my office in the
middle of the afternoon?"

I looked pointedly at the clock over his desk. He followed my gaze, a look of surprise crossing his face as he
realized it was nearly five.

"Okay, late in the afternoon."

Wade got up and walked around his desk. He put a
hand on my left shoulder. "You look upset," he said. "What
happened?"

This was my moment of truth. Either I trusted Wade,
and I told him what happened, or I walked away.

Decision time, Neverall.

"What we found, it's bad, Wade. Real bad."

He crouched down until he was at eye level. His hand
slid off my shoulder and rested on my arm. He reached
for my right hand, and held it.

"What did the sheriff say, Georgie? Did he tell you
anything?"

"It's blood. Like that's any big surprise. I mean, you

saw it, right? We all knew what it was. And those shell casings." I shook myself, trying to throw off the image.

"But you knew all that before, and you said you were fine. Which you were, more or less. Something happened since then. Was it something the sheriff did?"

"Not exactly. I mean, it was stressful being in that office. And it didn't help that there was a reporter waiting for me, and I had to sneak out the back door to avoid him.

"But just before I left, the sheriff told me they had some results on the tests they were doing.

"I don't even know if I'm supposed to tell anyone, Wade, but I have to talk to somebody!"

Wade nodded, and waited silently for me to continue.

"It's the same blood type as Martha Tepper's."

I swallowed, and went on. "The sheriff says they'll run DNA tests, and they'll take a few days. But I think he's already sure."

The color drained from Wade's face, and he had to swallow a few times before he could speak again. "Sure that it's Martha's blood?" he asked. "Or sure that . . ."

He couldn't complete the thought.

"Both."

Wade gripped my hand so tightly I thought he might break my fingers. I frowned and he loosened his hold, muttering "Sorry."

"And that's not the worst of it."

Wade's expression said clearly that he couldn't think of anything much worse. His client, friend, and neighbor was missing, and her blood had been found in a place it didn't belong.

How much worse could it get?

"They picked up her housekeeper and took her to the sheriff's office."

I told him about running into Janis Breckweth and giving her a lift back to the Second Chances shelter.

"She's living there now," I said. "She cooks for them, and they gave her a place to stay. I guess it's sort of the

same deal she had with Miss Tepper, and she made sure
we all knew she was working there, not just staying at the
shelter.

"I don't think she had anything to do with this, Wade.
She didn't do anything except talk, and what she said
bothered me. A lot."

"Go on."

"She says she has a diary that Martha Tepper was
keeping the last few weeks before she disappeared."

I repeated the things Janis had told me, and her claims
that someone had been stealing from Miss Tepper.

"Janis said Martha suspected the Gladstones, that she
was making notes about things, and she was going to give
them a chance to fix things."

"She must have," Wade said.

"What do you mean? She didn't fix anything. Janis
was left without a job or a place to live, even though Martha promised to take care of her. And the Gladstones
are still in charge of her business affairs. And you're her
accountant—shouldn't you be worried about all this?"

"If there was some truth to it, I would be. But I don't
think there is."

Wade stopped. Some color had returned to his face,
and he had relaxed his grip on my hands. He studied my
face for seconds that felt like hours, then rolled his eyes.

"I cannot believe I'm going to do this," he said. "But I
have to trust you. You understand, everything I am going
to tell you is in strictest confidence. No one else knows
about this, except the people involved. Do I have your
word that you will not repeat this to anyone, for any reason?"

"But what if—"

"No *but*s, Georgie. You can't tell anyone."

"I promise."

"Martha Tepper made a loan to the Gladstones, just a
few weeks before she left. They were having some problems, like so many folks around here. They made some

bad investments and business was slow. The same problems everybody had, but they had gotten deeply into debt. Martha sent me a copy of the loan agreement, with instructions to put it in her file. It was a sizable loan, with very generous terms, but she could easily afford it. She said they would pay it back as soon as they could, and she was sure they were good for it. So whatever her dispute with Rick and Rachel was, she must have resolved it."

"Maybe," I said slowly. "But what if she started suspecting them after she made the loan? What if she gave them the money and then discovered that they had taken more than they were supposed to, or they weren't paying the bills they were supposed to, and they wouldn't be able to pay it back? Or what if—"

Wade let go of my hands and grabbed my shoulders. He gave me a gentle shake and shook his head. "That's a lot of *what-if*s, Georgie. There isn't any reason to believe any of it."

"But Janis said—"

"And Janis has every reason to resent the Gladstones. They were Martha's attorneys, sure. But they were also her friends, and she helped them out before she left.

"Janis expected to be helped, too, and that didn't happen. Instead, Rachel Gladstone showed up and told her she would have to move out of the house because it was being sold."

He stood up, releasing my shoulders, and paced across the small office. "She's angry, and maybe scared about her future. From her perspective, the Gladstones got all the things she was promised."

"But what about the diary?"

"What about it?" Wade held his hands out, palms up. "Have you seen it? Do you know where it is? Do you even know for sure that it exists?"

"Janis says it's in a safe place."

"Janis says. Janis says." He plopped back into his swivel chair behind the desk and leaned over the cluttered surface.

"She doesn't know who to trust, Wade. And really, can you blame her?"

"She doesn't know who to trust, but she expects *you* to trust *her*? Maybe she ought to trust the sheriff. She should give him what she has and let him do his job."

I sighed. There was no reason for us to be fighting about this. Wade was right, Janis *should* trust the sheriff. But she wasn't going to. Not as long as she was his prime suspect.

"I'll keep working on it," I said. "Maybe if she gives the diary to the sheriff, that will change his mind."

Wade nodded in agreement. "That sounds like a good idea, Georgie. Maybe you can convince her to tell the sheriff what she told you. And if she backs that up with an actual diary, then he'll have something to work with."

It wasn't much of a plan, but it was all I had. I'd make time tomorrow to talk to Janis again. If I could convince her to trust me, maybe I could get her to go to the sheriff with whatever she had.

"Feel better?" Wade asked. He stood again, came around the desk, and held out his hand to help me up from the chair. "Been a long day, Georgie. You could use some food and a beer.

"I'm buying."

"A quick one," I said. "The dogs are waiting for me and I promised them a long walk. And," I admitted, "I'm beat."

"How about this?" Wade shut down his computer and started putting away the files that were scattered across the top of his old-fashioned wooden desk. "You go let the dogs out, and I'll be at your place in twenty minutes with Tiny's burgers and some microbrew. I'll help you walk the dogs after we eat."

"Now that's an offer too good to turn down." I smiled up at Wade and turned for the door, digging my car keys out of my pocket.

I stopped and turned back around. "But those had better be double cheeseburgers," I said. "I didn't get much lunch, and I'm starved!"

Wade grinned and waved me out of the office as he switched off the desk lamp.

"See you in twenty."

I debated a shower while the dogs visited the backyard, but I decided against it. Whatever my thing was with Wade—and I was beginning to think it actually might be a thing—it wasn't at the answer-the-door-in-my-bathrobe point. Yet.

Wade, I was discovering, was much prompter than Sue. While I could count on Sue's twenty minutes being at least thirty, Wade's twenty was closer to eighteen.

I did manage to comb my hair and grab a clean T-shirt before he knocked on the front door.

True to his word, he had a bag of double cheeseburgers, with fries, from Tiny's, and a six-pack.

It wasn't the kind of meal I used to eat. Two years ago I would have been horrified at the carb count of the microbrew, and the burger wouldn't have had a slab of melted cheese on top.

But I'd left that girl in San Francisco, and the woman who lived in Pine Ridge liked her burgers with gooey cheese and fries and beer.

The woman who lived in Pine Ridge worked at a job she loved and ate what she liked. She kept her weight in check with hard work instead of a high-priced fitness center, and she dressed in jeans and comfortable shoes.

I was starting to really enjoy being that woman.

After dinner, we clipped the leashes to the dogs' collars and set out for our walk. Wade was pleasant company and we carefully avoided the topic of Martha Tepper and the people around her.

For that one hour, walking in the cool summer evening, I could pretend that I'd only seen stars, and the rising moon, and all I'd heard was the breeze stirring the branches of the evergreens along our route.

I couldn't keep the illusion, though, once Wade left. It was still early and I was too keyed up to sleep.

The dogs settled into their beds, having wolfed down

their treats, and I wandered around the house. I loaded the dishwasher and started it running. I stripped the bed and remade it with clean sheets.

After all that had happened, I kept thinking about how much my life had changed in the few months I'd been back in Pine Ridge.

Once again, I pulled out my gi. The routines calmed me as I moved through them. I thought about the empty storefront on Main Street.

I wasn't ready to give up my martial arts training, but I didn't think I wanted to be a teacher.

Besides, I had discovered plumbing, and as silly as it sounded, I really enjoyed my job. When I left high tech, I had wanted something as far removed as I could find, and plumbing seemed to fit the bill. Yet in some ways, it was a lot like computer programming. Except you moved water instead of data.

It was hard work and you got dirty—a lot—and it was too hot in the summer and way too cold in the winter. But there was something about it that gave me a sense of accomplishment. The longer I worked with Barry, the more I realized it was where I belonged.

I reached the end of my workout and dragged myself to the shower. I tumbled into bed. Tired, still worried about Martha Tepper, but at least I had a plan.

It was good to be home.

In the morning, Barry was waiting by his pickup when I arrived. He looked at his watch, then back at me. I shook my head and tapped the face of my watch. According to my beat-up drugstore timepiece, I was right on time.

Barry watched me climb out of the Beetle. Whatever he was planning to say was short-circuited when I handed him a steaming mocha from the espresso place a few blocks away.

Barry sipped, and flinched when the scalding liquid hit his tongue. "Mmmm," he hummed. "Tell me this is sugar-free, please. Paula is all over my case about sugar, so I promised to drink sugar-free mochas."

I screwed up my face in an expression of disgust. A lot of things were okay in their sugar-free versions, but chocolate wasn't one of them.

"Of course it is," I lied. "Wouldn't want you crossing Paula—she'd take you apart."

Barry chuckled and took another careful sip. "She could."

"Lucky for you, she's crazy about you. So you're safe, at least for now."

We carried our coffee inside the echoing space of the warehouse. There hadn't been any work done inside since the day we'd discovered Martha Tepper's brooch in the drain pipe of the utility sink.

I realized with a start that it had only been a couple weeks, although it felt a lot longer.

I looked around. The drain for the utility sink was still disassembled, a rag stuffed in the end of the pipe to block any sewer gas from getting into the building.

"Where do you want to start?" I asked.

Barry thought for a minute, then said, "The bathroom. If we can get that working, it would be a good thing. Customers are always happier if the toilet's working."

I nearly answered with a slang expression, but I stopped myself just in time. Even a bad pun wasn't justification for breaking Barry's cursing rule. And bringing him his favorite mocha didn't earn me a free pass, either.

"Me, too."

Barry chuckled. He was learning about having a woman on the job site, just as I was learning to work with an all-male crew.

True, my crew at Samurai Security had been nearly all male, but a computer security company was a far cry from a construction site. There were certain amenities that you took for granted in an office.

The toilet was a challenge, but we finally got it working properly and started in on the trough sink that ran along one wall. The urinals could wait until later.

We had replaced the valve seats on two of the faucets, and had four more to go, when I heard the ominous tapping that signaled the appearance of Sandra Neverall.

The tapping drew closer, and she called out to us.

"Mr. Hickey? Georgiana? Where are you?"

"Working in the bathroom, Ms. Neverall," Barry answered. "Hang on a minute, we'll be right out."

"Please don't interrupt yourselves on my account," she said. "I just wanted to talk to you for a—Oh!"

Sandra stopped just inside the bathroom door, staring at the row of urinals that lined the opposite wall. Her face colored, and I expected her to beat a hasty retreat.

But once again, I underestimated Sandra Neverall. She stood her ground, and in a few seconds she had her expression, and her color, under tight control.

"So, Mr. Hickey. Can you give me some idea when you'll be able to finish up the house? We really need to keep that project moving, and I know you're the one to ask." She smiled sweetly, an expression so clearly fake I nearly choked.

I had to give Barry points for cool, though. He didn't rise to her bait. "Well, in this case," he said, "I'm afraid I don't have much say over when we can get back to work. That will be up to the sheriff. As soon as he lets us back in, we'll make that our top priority."

"So, I need to talk to the sheriff, then. I see."

"Yep." Barry turned his attention back to the faucet he was disassembling. "Once he gives us the go-ahead, we should be able to wrap up the job in a day. Maybe two, if we don't find any surprises." He paused. "I sincerely hope we've had all the surprises we're going to have on that job."

"I do, too," Sandra said tartly.

She finally turned to me. "Are you all right, Georgiana? I heard the sheriff made you come to the station, or whatever it is. Gregory said he questioned my daughter like a common criminal!"

I wasn't sure whether her outrage was for me, or for the damage it might do to her reputation.

"I was actually an *uncommon* criminal, Mother. I was innocent."

Her sour expression told me my flip attitude wasn't making things any better.

"Really, Mom, it wasn't like that. The sheriff asked me to come down to his office and talk to him about what I found. All I did was answer some questions and tell him what happened. Then he sent me home. End of excitement."

"But you went back!"

"Yes. I told him about Martha Tepper's brooch and he asked if I would bring it in. I went back, gave it to the deputy, and that was the end of it."

Something was bothering me. "Did you say Gregory told you all this?"

"Yes. Over dinner last night. We met the Gladstones at the steak house. They hadn't heard what happened, so that was the major topic of conversation, as you can well imagine. Anyway, Gregory heard about it from an associate in his office, who has a friend in the sheriff's office. I believe what the young man actually said was, 'I didn't know they made pretty plumbers.' Or something like that." She waved dismissively. "At any rate, Gregory told us everything he had heard. Which, by the way"—she raised one eyebrow, an expression she knew made me crazy— "was much more than I heard from my own daughter."

"Well, Mother, I didn't have a friend in the sheriff's department to give me inside information. All I knew was that the sheriff asked me questions and I answered them."

"Excuse me, Ms. Neverall," Barry broke in.

Mother and I both turned to him.

"Yes?"

"Yes?"

She spoke a fraction of a second before me, the effect like the echo of an audio delay loop.

"We need to get back to work here, Georgie," Barry said. "If you'll excuse us, Ms. Neverall." There was a glint of amusement in his eyes. He carefully avoided looking directly at my mother. "We'll get back to work on the house just as soon as Sheriff Mitchell allows us."

Sandra clicked back into business mode. She could sure take a hint. "Naturally, Mr. Hickey. I'll check with the sheriff's office and see if he has any timetable on when that might be."

She opened the door and stepped into the hall as her cell phone rang. She tapped her Bluetooth headset and answered crisply, "Sandra Neverall, Whitlock Associates. What can I do to help you?"

She waved over her shoulder without looking back. I listened as her heels clicked across the warehouse floor, echoing in the empty space, until the outside door closed behind her.

"Thanks, Barry."

He shrugged. "We did need to get back to work. And there wasn't anything I could tell her that would help. Like I said, nothing we can do until the sheriff releases the house."

We worked through the morning, finishing the faucets. By the time we broke for lunch, every tap along the sink was working perfectly and sealing tight. Like I said, a feeling of accomplishment.

Barry lowered the tailgate of his truck and grabbed his lunch sack out of the front seat. I left him sitting in the sun and made a quick drive through the local sandwich shop. I told myself turkey on rye would make up for the burger and fries last night, and I almost believed it.

I drove home to let the dogs out and stood at the kitchen counter to eat my sandwich. If I couldn't talk Janis into giving the diary to the sheriff, there had to be some other way to prove it existed. I just had to find the proof.

Too bad I hadn't been able to search all of Miss Tepper's things before they were loaded on the truck. If that darned toilet hadn't fallen on my leg, things would have been better. I could have looked in—

I *had* looked in the china hutch! I thought back. I'd

pulled open the drawers, and there had been something in the back of one of them.

A scrap of paper.

I remembered sticking it in my pocket when I heard Sean coming back in the house, but I didn't remember seeing it after that. What had I done with it?

Nothing. I'd gone to the clinic and then come home, dumping my work clothes into the hamper in the garage.

My dirty laundry was spilling over the top of the hamper onto the floor. For once I was grateful I'd neglected to wash it. The paper might still be in the pocket of those jeans.

I rooted through the pile one-handed, the turkey sandwich still clutched in my other hand. Halfway down, I found the jeans. I dug in the pocket and felt something stiff and scratchy.

I had it!

It was the corner of a sheet of heavy paper, more like parchment. Like the paper in a fancy diary.

There were only a few words on the scrap I held, but the handwriting looked like Martha Tepper's precise penmanship. It might be the proof I needed.

The word *Gladstone* was clearly written there, but the paper was torn next to the name. There was no way to know which Gladstone she was referring to, though from what I'd seen, they were practically inseparable. To think, I'd had a bit of Martha's diary the entire time—and now it was part of an important piece of evidence.

Combined with what Janis had told me, it might be enough to give the sheriff a starting point. Now if I could just get the diary from her.

Wade had defended the Gladstones, but there had to be something he didn't know. I was certain he was wrong.

From the backyard, I heard frantic barking and the scrabbling sound of eight canine feet dashing up the back steps. I ran into the kitchen, just in time to see Daisy and Buddha race back into the house, dripping wet. They stopped in the middle of the floor to shake themselves, then ran back outside.

My sandwich was covered with drops of what I hoped was water, and I suddenly lost my appetite. I dropped my food on the counter and ran out the door after the dogs.

Running under the fence from my neighbor's yard was a stream of dark brown water. I stood on tiptoe and peered over the fence. The neighbor's hose snaked through the rows of his garden, with a steady flow of water coming from the end.

The water had soaked the garden and begun to run off down the slope that led to my yard, where Daisy and Buddha were now rolling merrily in the newly created mud.

I tried not to think about what they had just splattered all over my kitchen. Especially since there was no time to clean it up before I went back to work.

The dogs grinned up at me, pleased with their newfound game. They were both a mess of mud and matted hair, and they desperately needed baths. But I needed to get back to the warehouse.

I ran next door and pounded on the door. I hurriedly yelled at Mr. Stevens, who was rather hard of hearing, that his garden was overwatered, and he needed to shut the hose off.

He apologized and said he'd fallen asleep, but I was halfway back to my front door by the time he finished his sentence.

Once inside again, I grabbed the phone and hit the speed dial for Doggy Day Spa. When Sue answered, I blurted out, "Airedale emergency, girl. They're covered in mud and I need to get back to work ASAP. Have you got time for a couple shampoos this afternoon?"

"Sure. But you have to promise a full explanation when you pick them up." She laughed. "And it better be good."

"You bet," I answered. "Be there in five."

I hung up without saying good-bye, dragged the dogs into the garage, and wiped them down with some old towels I kept for rainy days. This was close enough.

Buddha accepted his hasty scrubbing with his usual

calm manner, but Daisy was highly offended that I had interrupted her playtime. It was, she implied, a perfectly reasonable occupation for an Airedale, and I was just being mean.

"Stop pouting," I told her as I bundled them into the car. "You're the one that insisted on rolling in the mud. Now you need to go see Sue."

At the name *Sue*, both dogs scrambled for the backseat. "Traitors," I muttered, slamming the door behind them and moving around to the driver's door.

I dropped them at Sue's, enduring her amusement at their muddy coats, and jumped back in the car. I was pushing it, and after this morning I didn't want to be late again. Especially without a mocha peace offering.

I pulled into the warehouse parking lot with several minutes to spare and parked next to Barry's pickup. At first I thought he must be back in the building, but the tailgate of the truck was still down.

When I looked in the back, Barry was flaked out, his head propped on his rolled-up jacket, snoozing in the sun.

I almost hated to wake him. But then he snored and I couldn't stop a giggle. He sat up, his expression still sleepy, and looked around for the source of the noise.

"Nice nap?" I asked with mock innocence.

"You're late," he growled.

"Been standing here watching you sleep," I countered. "You missed all the excitement."

"Nothing exciting happened here."

"Not here, at my house. Come on, let's get to work. I'll tell you the whole story."

By the time I'd finished my tale of doggy woe, Barry was chuckling. "Don't laugh," I told him. "You get that Jack Russell for Paula, you're going to have plenty of stories of your own. Jack Russells are high-energy dogs."

"I know." Barry shook his head. "But what Paula wants . . ."

"Paula gets," I finished.

We went to work on the urinals. By midafternoon, I

could see that Barry was running down. He moved slowly and he was still favoring his right leg.

"Barry," I said in my most innocent voice, "what did Dr. Cox say when you went to Immediate Care?"

There was a long pause, which answered the question I was *really* asking. Barry hadn't gone to the doctor at all, despite his promises.

"I intended to go, Georgie. But I stopped at the office to get the paperwork, and the next thing I knew, it was after five." He shrugged. "I was sure the doc had gone home already, so I figured I'd stop in the next morning, but then I got busy."

It was my turn to glare at him. "You promised, Barry." This was one of those more-brother-than-boss moments, and I propped my fists on my hips. "So when are you going to go?"

"Okay, okay. I'll stop by after work. All right?"

I grinned at him and he gave me a sour look. "Bad enough I have a woman bossing me around at home," he said. "This is what I get for letting one on the job."

"And you're Megan's hero because of it." I reminded him of his daughter's pointed questions about why there were no women plumbers in his company.

The work on the urinals was complete. All that was left to do was clean up the job site. Barry's rule.

"It's almost five, Barry. Maybe you ought to go now, so you don't miss the doctor."

He opened his mouth, but I continued before he could speak. "I'll even do the cleanup if you promise to go by the clinic. Deal?"

It was an offer too good to refuse, and we both knew it. Cleanup was always a chore, one nobody really wanted to do. And I was offering to do it all.

I was picking up tools and fitting them into the boxes when I heard Barry's truck drive away. I smiled to myself. He was a great person to work for, but he was such a guy sometimes. Good thing he had Paula to look out for him.

As I worked, I thought about Barry's accident. We'd

made a joke about the job being jinxed, but it had me spooked; especially after we found the bloody towel.

What if the stair hadn't been an accident? Maybe someone really wanted to stop our work on the house; maybe they were afraid we would find exactly what we did find in the basement.

Maybe the cracked toilet wasn't an accident, either.

I felt in my pocket for the scrap of paper I'd found before the dogs' adventure. I had intended to take it to the sheriff, but Daisy and Buddha had foiled my clever plan.

I decided I would stop by the sheriff's office after I finished cleaning up, and show him my clue. Then I could ask about the stairs. Maybe they had already looked at it, but it never hurt to ask, did it?

I heard a vehicle pull into the parking lot. Had Barry left too late to see the doctor? Or had he been to the clinic and back in the time it took me to clean up? I glanced at my beat-up watch. Had it really been that long?

The outside door opened and footsteps echoed through the empty warehouse.

"Still back here," I called out, bending down to put the last of my tools in my toolbox. "What did you forget? Whatever it is, it could have waited 'til morning."

"No," a smooth voice said. "I don't think it could have."

chapter 22

The voice wasn't Barry's. It was Rick Gladstone's.

"We saw your little car, and thought we'd stop in to say good-bye."

Rick and Rachel stood in the door of the bathroom.

With a gun.

Pointed at me.

Rachel held the gun in her right hand. It wasn't a very big gun, but at that instant it was the only thing I could see.

Her hand trembled slightly, and she wrapped her left hand around her right to steady her grip.

I stood up very slowly, my hands held out to my sides. I kept my face calm and didn't speak.

I'd learned how to defend myself. But I also knew trying to disarm a nervous person with a gun was a good way to get yourself seriously killed. Especially when you were outnumbered, and your opponent had the element of surprise.

And I was surprised.

As I'd said to Barry a few days earlier, you choose your battles. I wasn't ready to choose this one quite yet.

"Rachel." Rick struggled to keep his voice level and smooth, but I could hear an edge of fear underneath. "How do we get rid of her?"

Anger flashed across Rachel's face, and for a split second I thought she was going to pull the trigger.

"Well, we can't just shoot her, can we? Not unless you're prepared to dig up Martha and put them together."

I had a sudden image of being thrown on top of Martha Tepper's body. I shuddered, unable to help myself.

"Don't worry, you'd already be dead," Rachel said.

Somehow I didn't find that very reassuring.

Rachel stood still for one long minute, clearly trying to formulate a plan. I realized that these two had come after me on impulse, without a clear idea of what they would do when they found me.

Sort of like a dog chasing a car, but with deadly consequences for the car.

I watched Rick watching Rachel, and realized that he was not in charge of this operation. I wondered if he had ever been in charge. Of anything.

Then again, Rachel didn't seem like much of a leader.

"So," I said, drawing her attention away from her planning, and back to me, "if you really plan to kill me, would you at least tell me why? I mean, I get that you two were stealing from Martha's accounts. That was what this was all about, right?"

Rachel's mouth clamped shut, her bottom lip caught between her small teeth. She was determined not to talk, not to give away anything.

But Rick wanted to defend himself.

"It wasn't like that." The whine I had heard before surfaced, and I forced myself not to show the revulsion and contempt I felt.

"It wasn't?" I said.

"No! We didn't steal anything. We borrowed some money from one of the trust accounts. Just to take care of some office bills. We would eventually have billed her for it anyway. We just got the money a little early."

"And Martha objected?" I asked.

"We only took what she promised us," Rachel cut in, her voice harsh. "We were having trouble, were about to lose our house. The old biddy said she'd help us out. Then she started talking about that charity housing project and how maybe she ought to give the money to them."

"But she'd already promised us," Rick whined, "and she had plenty. She wouldn't even have missed it if she hadn't gotten the idea in her head to move."

"We really were going to pay her back. We even signed a note," Rachel said. "But she wouldn't believe us."

"Why not?" I said. I just wanted to keep them talking instead of shooting, until I could figure out a way to get out of the warehouse.

Rick launched into a long explanation about how they had been getting shortchanged by Martha for years, and they had been forced to pad their bills and siphon funds from Martha's trust accounts.

"It was her own fault," Rachel snarled. "If she hadn't been so cheap, we could have worked it all out. But she insisted that we had to turn ourselves in even after we signed the note to pay some of it back.

"For what?" she exploded. "For taking what should have been ours in the first place? Just because she was rich, Miss High-and-Mighty Martha Tepper, did that give her the right to treat us like dirt? To make us lose our house and our business?" Her voice rose with indignation. "To make us go to *jail*?"

Maybe I had pushed her too far. She was trembling, and the gun clenched in her fists was waving around the room as though looking for any random target.

"This is your own fault, you know." She waved the gun, the barrel still pointing at the middle of my chest. "If you had just left things alone, we could have taken care of the situation. But *nooo*. Not you! You had to keep poking around the house, and talking to that stupid housekeeper, and running to the sheriff every five minutes."

I didn't see any advantage in pointing out how wrong she was, so I kept my mouth shut.

"We tried to warn you," she continued. "That first night? With the truck? You didn't get the message. Then the missing tools. We hoped you'd stop getting into things at the house. I even fixed the toilet so it would break and you would have to stop work, but you didn't. And we tried to fix the basement stairs to keep you out of there, too, until we'd had a chance to get rid of some things."

I thought about the truck that had tried to run me off the road. Had Rachel been driving, or Rick? My money was on Rachel. Not that it mattered.

I wondered if there had been more than the bag we found. It was possible there were other things, either in the walls or stashed in one of the crates or boxes that were in storage.

Rachel seemed to be working herself up, building her justification for taking the next step.

Which, I was very much afraid, would be firing a bullet in my direction.

Rick apparently had the same thought. He put his arm around his wife's shoulders and steadied the gun, the barrel pointing toward the floor.

"It was an accident," Rick said, back on the defensive. "We only meant to scare her into signing a note for another loan, giving us the money we needed. I took that stupid old brooch and told her she could have it back when she signed the note. We still planned to pay it back, not like we were trying to rob her or anything. But she kept telling us we had to go to the police, had to give ourselves up. Like we'd done something really bad. I threw the brooch in the sink. Just so she would know we were serious. Rachel *told* her to sign but she wouldn't. She said she was going to the police if we didn't, and then she started to walk out." He patted his wife's shoulder, pulling her against his chest as though to comfort her.

I relaxed a fraction. For the first time since they had entered the room, the gun was no longer pointed directly at me.

I wasn't ready to move, but now I at least had a chance.

"We were just trying to stop her." His voice was choked with regret, though whether over the shooting of Miss Tepper or over getting caught, I wasn't sure.

I was voting for getting caught. He didn't seem like the type of guy to have much compassion for anyone that wasn't him.

"We worked too hard to get where we were," Rachel said, as though that justified everything they had done. "Did you know I put Rick through law school?"

The abrupt change of subject reminded me of one of Sue's roller-coaster conversations.

If Sue was a homicidal maniac, holding me at gunpoint.

I hoped Sue was taking good care of the dogs. If I didn't get out of here, she was going to inherit a couple Airedales instead of getting that Great Dane she'd been thinking about.

The thought that I might never see Daisy and Buddha again tore at my heart. The two of them had helped me through the roughest time of my life, and I owed them a lot.

No way were they going to be left orphans. And no way was I going to let myself get taken out by someone who whined as much as these two losers.

The time had come to choose my battle.

I judged the distance between me and the Gladstones. They were several feet away, but I was already standing. I had never tried any martial arts moves in steel-toed boots, but I was about to find out if I could.

I couldn't move directly toward them. All either one of them would have to do was raise the gun and fire. At close range, moving toward the gun—like I said, you could get seriously dead.

I tensed, and mentally chose my spot, aiming for the wall a few feet beyond Rick Gladstone.

Go time.

I bounced once and tumbled toward Rick. He jumped and pulled at the gun, but by the time he managed to swing it around toward me, I was behind him. I landed awkwardly in the heavy boots and bounced off the wall.

My shoulder thudded into the door of the one toilet stall and it swung wildly, metal clanging against metal. The noise reverberated off the tile and concrete of the bathroom, sending echoes vibrating through the room.

Rachel screamed. She relinquished control of the gun to Rick and clapped her hands over her ears.

I landed in a crouch and launched myself at Rick's knees.

He had the gun, and that made him my main target.

I blocked out the sound of Rachel's screams.

Knees are a vulnerable spot when your opponent is standing. I focused on Rick. On his knees.

I saw the gun in his hand as I slid into Rick's legs.

One boot, the steel toe a weapon in its own right, smashed into his left knee and he went down.

I heard the deep boom of a gunshot next to my ear and felt a streak of searing heat tear across the back of my neck.

A tile shattered a few feet away, sending sharp slivers of broken ceramic flying. I felt the sting of the tiny shards cutting into my arms and face.

I saw the gun clatter away, knocked from Rick's hand by the force of his fall.

He moved to crawl after it. His face contorted in agony, and I felt a guilty stab of satisfaction.

There was something near my eye, and I reached up to wipe it off. I pulled my hand away covered with blood from the cuts on my face.

I scrambled after the gun. I knew the cuts were superficial, but there were a lot of them, each one bleeding just enough to leave a red smear on anything I touched.

I grabbed the gun with slick fingers, fumbling madly for a button of some kind. I knew some guns had a safety that would prevent them from firing, and I sincerely did not want that gun to fire again.

Rachel Gladstone smashed down on top of me.

"You hurt my Rick!" she screamed. Her fingernails raked my arms as she grappled for the gun.

"Your Rick was trying to shoot me!" I screamed back.

Rachel grabbed me by the hair, pulling with all her might.

I twisted and turned her hold against her, forcing her hand back until the pain was too much and she let go.

The gun clattered away and I scuttled after it.

Rick was still moving, his face twisting with each motion.

I skirted around him, trying to reach the gun, to keep it away from both of them.

Rachel grabbed my ankles and tried to pull me back. I kicked her squarely in the face, and was rewarded with the crack of a broken nose.

I turned around knowing that sound meant she was out of action, at least for a while. Unfortunately, I found the gun once again pointed at my chest.

Rick, his face a mask of pain and anger, held the weapon steady.

The rest of the world dropped away, and there was only the two of us. And the gun.

"Rachel was right about you. You're way more trouble than you're worth," he said.

I sent a silent apology to Daisy and Buddha and Sue. At least they would have each other. I thought for an instant of Wade, and whether we would really have been a thing.

And of my mother. She didn't understand me, but she loved me, and I wouldn't have the chance to tell her I loved her, too.

I couldn't focus on the gun any longer. I couldn't focus on anything. My ears still rang from the noise of the shot in the small room.

I closed my eyes, and exhaustion flowed over me. No matter how hard I fought, it was over. And I knew it.

I heard a distant voice yell, "Drop the weapon."

"I don't have a weapon," I whispered, without opening my eyes.

I wished I did. Then maybe Rick wouldn't be able to shoot me.

As I heard footsteps rushing toward us, it still didn't occur to me that I wasn't dead.

chapter 23

"I still say you should be in the hospital," my mother said as she fussed with the blanket I'd tossed aside.

She folded it carefully, and draped it artfully across the arm of the sofa.

"Are you sure there isn't anything else I can get for you?" she asked. For about the hundredth time.

"Really, Mom, I'm okay."

I smiled up at her. I really was okay—even though I had scratches and nicks on my arms, face, and neck from the broken tile, and a second-degree burn across the back of my neck.

My hearing had quickly returned to normal, though, and I had never felt better in my life. Which, it seemed, I was going to be allowed to continue living.

Mom fussed a few minutes longer, then relented.

"Call me if you need anything, Georgiana. You know"— she didn't look at me and her voice dropped to little more than a whisper—"you could come and stay with me, if you'd like."

I actually considered her offer.

"No, Mom. But thanks. You need your space, just like I need mine. We'd be at each other's throats within an hour."

She grinned at me—not the usual Sandra cool smile, but an amused twitch of her mouth—and nodded. "Probably right. But you call if you need me, okay?"

"I will. But I'll be fine. Sue's due any minute with the dogs, and Wade's bringing pizza."

The momentary truce ended and a look of horror crossed my mother's face. "Do you think you're up to having those rambunctious dogs around while you're recovering?"

"They're pretty mellow, Mom. And I'm not an invalid."

Her arched eyebrow told me she didn't agree, but she was learning not to argue with me. Especially when I was right.

Mom left and I leaned back, carefully arranging a pillow behind me so that nothing touched my neck. Dr. Cox had warned me I might have to sleep on my stomach for a few days while the burn healed.

I couldn't explain to her that I needed to be home with the dogs. That they had been what gave me the determination to fight back when Rick and Rachel held that gun on me.

But as much as I loved Daisy and Buddha, I knew I needed more than a couple Airedales in my life. My mother was part of what I needed, and I didn't have the words to explain it to her right now.

More than anything, though, I wanted to know what happened.

Sheriff Mitchell had refused to talk to me when I came to, insisting I go with the paramedics and get checked out.

When I'd finished with Dr. Cox, I tried to go to the sheriff's office. A knot of reporters waited at the front door, so I parked around back and called Deputy Carruthers.

Carruthers was polite, but he flatly refused to let me in the back door. "The sheriff said the doctor told you to go home and rest. He'll talk to you when he's through processing the Gladstones. And it isn't worth my job to let you in." I could hear the grin in his voice as he spoke the last sentence.

I gave up and headed home, where I found Mother's Escalade parked at the curb and Mother waiting to fuss over me.

Now that she was gone, I was anxious to see Sue and Wade. Maybe they could fill me in.

Wade, Sue, Daisy, and Buddha showed up together. Sue had the dogs on their leashes, freshly bathed and combed, and Wade carried a couple of extra-large Garibaldi's boxes.

"Don't let them out back," I told Sue as she took the dogs off their leashes. "I haven't had a chance to take care of that mud, and I can't afford to have you bathe them again today."

Sue nodded. She tossed them a green treat and they settled in their beds. It had been a big day for them and they were ready for a snooze.

Wade came and sat next to me, taking my hands in his. "I owe you an apology, Georgie. I should have taken you seriously when you came to me with your suspicions. The worst part is, I wanted to believe you. I never liked the Gladstones much. But I was afraid that was coloring my judgment, so instead I continued to give them the benefit of the doubt long past the point I should have."

"And I wanted to believe it was Gregory, because of his relationship with my mother." I shrugged. "We were both wrong."

Sue brought plates and napkins from the kitchen, and we dug into the pizza.

"Aren't two extra-large a bit much for three people?" I asked before taking a big bite of pepperoni.

"Barry and Paula may drop by," Sue said.

"And Fred Mitchell," Wade added. "He wanted to talk to you. He said the reporters had them surrounded and there was no way he wanted you in the middle of that."

"What about the Gladstones? Where are they?" I never wanted to see either of them again, but I needed reassurance they were behind bars.

"They were a little beat-up," Wade said. "Don't suppose you'd care to explain that, would you?" He waited, and when I didn't answer, he went on. "Didn't think so. Anyway, the paramedics checked them over and released them to the sheriff. He booked them here, but he had to transfer Rachel into Portland. No place to hold a female prisoner here."

"That's because they need a woman on the force. And after what you did to the Gladstones, I'll bet he'd hire *you*, Georgie," Sue teased, then burst out laughing. "Deputy Georgie! Boy, if you thought your mom had trouble with you as a plumber . . ." She collapsed into a fit of laughter.

There was a knock at the front door and Sue jumped up to answer it. She returned a few seconds later with Sheriff Mitchell right behind her.

"How are you doing, Miss Neverall?" he asked politely.

"Fine, Sheriff. And it's Georgie. Grab a seat and a piece of pizza. You might as well get comfortable, because I expect the full story."

Sheriff Mitchell chuckled and settled into a chair. He accepted a plate from Sue and sniffed appreciatively. "Garibaldi's?"

"Yes, but you have to sing for your supper."

He took a bite, chewed, and swallowed before he pulled out his notebook and recorder and started asking questions.

No one had heard the story of what happened in the warehouse before, and I could see astonishment on Sue's face, and consternation on Wade's, as I recounted the story for the sheriff and his recorder.

"And that's when I heard someone say, 'Drop your weapon,' but I didn't have a weapon to drop," I said.

"That was me," Sheriff Mitchell said. "Thanks to your

friends here"—he indicated Wade and Sue—"we arrived in time."

"Like the cavalry riding to the rescue," I joked, trying to lighten the mood. Wade, I could see, didn't appreciate my feeble attempt at humor.

I had to ask, though I was sure I knew the answer to my question. "And they," I said softly, "killed Martha Tepper."

"No question," Sheriff Mitchell said. "As soon as we took them into custody, they started pointing the finger at each other. So much for sticking together. They claim they were just trying to frighten her, so she wouldn't turn them in. And they were angry because she wouldn't give them any more money. Rachel shot her, and Rick hid the body. He told us where and I have a crew out there now, recovering her remains." He shook his head, as though trying to dislodge the image.

"But how did you guys"—I looked at Wade and Sue—"manage to convince the sheriff?"

"The dogs," said Sue.

"The diary," said Wade.

"You didn't pick up the dogs when you said you would," Sue said. "When I couldn't reach you, I called Wade."

"I'd been thinking about what you said." Wade picked up the story. "I went to Second Chances and managed to talk Janis Breckweth into showing me the diary." He grinned at me. "I finally had to tell her I was your boyfriend, since you seemed to be the only person she trusted. As soon as I saw it, I knew it was Martha's, and I convinced her to let me take it to the sheriff."

Mitchell gave me a rare smile. "When we realized you were out there alone, I went out to check. Fortunately, I brought a few friends with me."

epilogue

We buried Martha Tepper a week later, in the family plot on a hill overlooking Pine Ridge.

As I looked around the faces of the crowd, I realized Pine Ridge was where I belonged. I had made the right choice in moving back, in spite of everything that had happened over the last few weeks.

I saw my mother reach for Gregory's hand as they stood at the graveside, and I realized how difficult this must be for her. She hadn't attended a funeral since we buried my father. We might never have an ideal relationship, but we both deserved the opportunity to try.

Standing between Wade and Sue, I began to feel the faint stirrings of trust, something I thought was dead forever.

Barry and Paula stood in for Miss Tepper's family, and Paula spoke lovingly of her dear friend. I wished I had known her better, and I felt a stab of regret that I would never have that chance.

After the service, as the crowd dwindled, I made my way to Paula's side.

"That was lovely," I said.

Paula nodded. "I'm really going to miss her." Her eyes were moist but she smiled faintly, as though she had a happy secret.

"Did you hear about the will?" she asked.

I shook my head. I knew the sheriff had found a will along with the diary Janis had rescued from the house, but beyond that, I hadn't heard anything.

"She left a generous bequest to the library, and one to Homes for Hope.

"The rest of it she left to Janis."

I smiled.

top ten tools for most home repairs

by georgiana neverall

I've learned the hard way to be prepared. My life spins out of control without the proper tools in hand. So here are the stripped-down basics I can't live without.

Some of these common tools are known by the name of the company that produces them (see Nos. 4, 5, 6, and 10).

1. Tape measure.

2. Hacksaw.

3. Rubber mallet.

4. Adjustable wrench (called by the brand name *Crescent*).

5. Slip-joint pliers (called by the brand name *Channellock*).

6. Locking-jaw pliers (called by the brand name *Vise-Grip*).

7. Plumber's snake or auger.

8. Toilet plunger.

9. Sink plunger.

10. Screwdrivers—flat blade (common) and Phillips, in an assortment of sizes. A multi-tip driver offers the convenience of an assortment in a compact space (such as the Nebo products).

One final note: If I ever find a tool (a legal one!) that will help me deal with my mother, I'm adding it to the list.

Cozy up with
Berkley Prime Crime

SUSAN WITTIG ALBERT
Don't miss the national bestselling series featuring herbalist China Bayles.

LAURA CHILDS
The Tea Shop Mysteries are the toast of Charleston, South Carolina.

KATE KINGSBURY
The Pennyfoot Hotel Mystery series is a teatime delight.

For the armchair detective in you.

penguin.com

Penguin Group (USA) Online

What will you be reading tomorrow?

Tom Clancy, Patricia Cornwell, W.E.B. Griffin,
Nora Roberts, William Gibson, Robin Cook,
Brian Jacques, Catherine Coulter, Stephen King,
Dean Koontz, Ken Follett, Clive Cussler,
Eric Jerome Dickey, John Sandford,
Terry McMillan, Sue Monk Kidd, Amy Tan,
John Berendt…

You'll find them all at
penguin.com

*Read excerpts and newsletters,
find tour schedules and reading group guides,
and enter contests.*

Subscribe to Penguin Group (USA) newsletters
and get an exclusive inside look
at exciting new titles and the authors you love
long before everyone else does.

PEN

M224G1107